# AMBUSH AT SODA CREEK

*Also by Lewis B. Patten*

GUNS AT GREY BUTTE

PROUDLY THEY DIE

GIANT ON HORSEBACK

THE ARROGANT GUNS

NO GOD IN SAGUARO

DEATH WAITED AT RIALTO CREEK

BONES OF THE BUFFALO

DEATH OF A GUNFIGHTER

THE RED SABBATH

THE YOUNGERMAN GUNS

POSSE FROM POISON CREEK

RED RUNS THE RIVER

A DEATH IN INDIAN WELLS

SHOWDOWN AT MESILLA

THE TRIAL OF JUDAS WILEY

THE CHEYENNE POOL

THE ORDEAL OF JASON ORD

BOUNTY MAN

LYNCHING AT BROKEN BUTTE

THE ANGRY TOWN OF PAWNEE BLUFFS

THE GALLOWS AT GRANEROS

# AMBUSH AT SODA CREEK

## LEWIS B. PATTEN

DOUBLEDAY & COMPANY, INC.
GARDEN CITY, NEW YORK
1976

All of the characters in this book are fictitious, and any relation
to actual persons, living or dead, is purely coincidental.

*First Edition*

ISBN: 0-385-11418-4
Library of Congress Catalog Card Number 75-25441
Copyright © 1976 by Lewis B. Patten
All Rights Reserved
Printed in the United States of America

# AMBUSH AT SODA CREEK

# CHAPTER 1

In midafternoon, the U. S. Army ambulance took a 45-degree left turn, following the deep-dust, two-track road, and the breeze, blowing from straight ahead now, cleared dust out of the vehicle, which was open both at front and rear, and brought a look of relief to the woman's weary face.

She sat facing sideways on the bench that ran along the right side of the ambulance. In other times and in another place, it would have been said of her that she was striking, even beautiful. Now, with dust caking her clothing and face and making her black hair look gray, the description did not apply.

Ahead, she could see the dusty, sweat-stained shirt back of the youthful driver and his uncut hair curling on his sunburned neck. His campaign hat was so dusty it looked gray instead of blue.

Beyond, she could see the backs of the four horses pulling the ambulance and beyond them two of the escort troopers riding fifty yards ahead. If she looked out behind she could see the ribbon of road they had traversed and the remaining two troopers bringing up the rear, far enough back so that they were out of the dust raised by the ambulance.

The heat was terrible. And although Stephanie Detrick hadn't seen a thermometer since leaving St. Louis, she knew the temperature must be at least a hundred and ten, which seemed almost unendurable, even allowing for the extreme dryness of the air. But now the breeze blowing through the vehicle evaporated her perspiration and temporarily made her feel cool. Or at least cooler by comparison.

She had come by Butterfield stagecoach from St. Louis to Lordsburg, where the ambulance, sent by her husband, Colonel Hans Detrick, and escorted by four troopers, had picked her up. From Lordsburg they had headed north and west into a land more desolate than any she had ever seen. They had been traveling for almost two days. Tonight, the troopers had told her, they ought to reach the fort.

Despite her exhaustion, despite the misery of the jolting ambulance and the heat, dust, and flies, there was no look of complaint on Stephanie Detrick's face. She was tired and she was numb. But this was a trip of her own choosing and she accepted the discomfort it entailed.

Various kinds of cactus dotted the barren landscape. Ocotillo, yucca. Sometimes a group of distant saguaros lifted their bare arms to the brassy sky as if in supplication. There was barrel cactus and the ubiquitous prickly pear. And always on all horizons were the mountains, made rose-violet by distance and very beautiful in their stark and barren way.

Rocks began to appear at the edges of the road, which had been traversing nearly level land before but which now began to dip into ravines and climb out again.

The attack came as a complete surprise, to Stephanie Detrick and to the troopers, who should have been expecting it or at least on the lookout for it.

It would not have made much difference whether they had been on guard or not. The outcome would have been the same. The troopers were outnumbered five to one by the squat, brown-skinned riders who came out of the rocks beside the road, galloping, yelling, firing with what at first seemed abandon at everything alive.

One of the lead troopers was first hit. He stood in his stirrups, dropped the reins, and clutched with both hands at his streaming throat. Blood spurted between his fingers for only an instant before he toppled from his horse, to lie still and crumpled in the rocks and dust at the side of the narrow road.

Stephanie Detrick stared at what was happening with startled unbelief. She had known this was Apache land. She had known her husband's command fought with the Indians. The presence of the four-man escort had told her there was some risk entailed just in traveling this road.

But it had happened so suddenly as to take her completely by surprise. The second lead trooper sagged sideways, shot through the chest. His horse bolted and he fell from his saddle. His foot caught in one stirrup and she last saw him being dragged by his galloping horse through the scrub brush and scattered rocks.

One of the four horses pulling the ambulance suddenly went down, shot through the neck. The vehicle stopped and the unhurt horses, driven wild by the smell of blood and by the noise, began kicking and fighting against the harness confining them.

Stephanie swung her head and looked behind. Both those troopers were valiantly trying to reach the ambulance, cut off as they now were by more than a dozen howling savages. One's horse, shot from under him, collapsed on the road, pinning the trooper's leg beneath his inert body. While the trooper was trying to extricate himself, he was brained by the butt of an Indian's gun.

The other trooper was literally riddled with bullets immediately afterward, still trying to get his carbine unslung from his back. The Indians caught his horse as he fell from the saddle. The dust cloud rolled forward and hid what happened afterward from Stephanie's gaze.

Not a bullet had touched the ambulance. The driver still sat its seat unhurt. He had no gun. If he had, he would probably have shot Stephanie and then himself.

Yanked off the seat of the ambulance, he was stunned but not killed by a blow to the head. Dark-skinned Apaches climbed into the ambulance and dragged Stephanie out. Their hands were not gentle but they made no attempt to injure her. She did not struggle, because she knew it would be a waste of time. They could kill her any time they chose with a single blow, a knife thrust, or a shot, and probably would if she gave them reason to.

Ungently she was boosted onto one of the downed troopers' horses. Her skirts were awkward but she sat astride. The Indians rode their horses away from the scene of the carnage at a walk, without even bothering to look back.

Stephanie Detrick was not a fool. She could only believe the purpose of this attack had been to kidnap her. She had to guess at the reasons for the kidnapping, but she assumed that in some way it involved her husband and his command at Fort Lincoln, now less than half a day away.

The four members of the escort had been killed; she didn't know it, but the driver had only been stunned by a blow to the head. The escort troopers' horses, those still uninjured, had been taken by the Indians but the horses that had been pulling the ambulance had been left behind.

Stephanie thought bleakly that she should have remained in St. Louis. Her failure to do so had cost all these lives, and she had an awful feeling that before this was over with, it was going to cost more.

What she did not realize was that this was war. She was

not the cause of it. Her coming had not started it. Nor would her staying away have prevented its continuance.

Private Samuel Roark was first conscious of a splitting headache. He opened his eyes, but closed them immediately because the brilliant sunlight made knives of pain shoot through his head. He was still for an instant while his mind groped for a memory of what had happened to him. Then, when it came, he struggled to his feet, ignoring the pain, and stared around.

The three living horses hitched to the ambulance now stood quietly, having worn themselves out in futile struggling. Green-bodied flies buzzed around the wound in the neck of the dead one, already laying their eggs in the drying blood. Roark staggered to the rear of the ambulance and stared into it, not knowing which would shock him most, to find Mrs. Detrick dead or to find her gone.

Finding her gone was probably the worst. He muttered, "Oh my God, I'll never get out of the stockade. The colonel will skin me alive for this!"

Turning, he saw Smith and Ives lying dead in the road behind the ambulance. Ives' leg was still pinned beneath the body of his horse.

Roark staggered to the front of the ambulance. Corporal Benjamin lay dead at the side of the road. Oliver Bell lay twenty or thirty yards from the road, where his foot had finally come loose from the stirrup.

The Indians were gone and Roark was the only one alive. He thought, "God Almighty, what am I gonna do?"

The smart thing to do would be to get on one of the horses and head south into Mexico. He started toward the horses but stopped when he remembered Mrs. Detrick. If he deserted now, it might be days before she was missed. They had been in Lordsburg more than a week, with orders to wait there for her as long as necessary, because the colonel hadn't known exactly when she would arrive.

Besides, how the hell could the colonel blame him for what had happened? He'd only been the driver. He hadn't even had a gun. It had been Corporal Benjamin's responsibility to see that the ambulance and Mrs. Detrick arrived safely at the fort.

Wincing occasionally from the excruciating pain in his head, Roark got out his knife and cut the harness of the dead horse, thinking as he did that the paymaster would probably take it out of his pay. He unhitched the horse from beside the dead one and led him off to the side of the road. The two remaining horses could pull the ambulance the rest of the way to the fort.

He went back along the road and, after working hard for several minutes, managed to free Ives' leg. He dragged the body to the ambulance. Straining and puffing, he finally got the man inside.

He returned for Smith, dragged him to the ambulance, and lifted him in too. The bodies were limp, which made loading them doubly difficult.

Circling the dead horse, he drove the ambulance forward along the road to a point just beyond where Corporal Benjamin lay. He loaded him, then went after Oliver Bell, and dragged him back to the road. When Bell's body had been loaded, he leaned against the side of the ambulance, bathed with sweat, panting with exhaustion, his head feeling like there were hammers inside it pounding against his skull. He wished he was dead but he wasn't and he had better get back to the fort as quickly as he could.

It never occurred to him that he had only been spared so

that he could carry word of the kidnapping to the fort. He supposed they had simply thought him dead.

From the position of the sun, he calculated that he had been unconscious for no more than an hour. He wanted to force the horses to trot but he did not. They had been on the road for two days. The two remaining horses were now pulling more weight than four had pulled before.

The third horse followed the ambulance about fifty yards behind. The world began to whirl in front of Roark's eyes. He knew he was going to lose consciousness, so he tied the reins loosely and crawled into the back of the ambulance. He collapsed. His head whirled briefly and then everything went black.

The horses were tired, but they knew hay, grain, and water waited for them at the fort. They didn't need to be driven. They continued at their steady, mile-eating walk toward Fort Lincoln as if Roark still was driving them.

The sun was down and the cloudless sky was yellow-orange when the ambulance finally arrived. An instant after it was sighted, the fort was in an uproar, but it was several minutes before it was discovered that Trooper Roark was still alive.

# CHAPTER 2

Captain Logan Garcia, crossing the parade, saw the ambulance as it came up out of the bed of Chiricahua Creek and approached the post. The horses walked slowly, their heads down. There was no driver on the seat.

Garcia felt an instant stab of concern. Only one ambulance was absent from the fort and it was due from Lordsburg with the colonel's wife. A four-man escort had been assigned to it.

He turned his head. "Corporal!"

The trooper turned and hurried toward him. Garcia said, "Tell Colonel Detrick that an ambulance is approaching." He himself was already running toward the driverless rig.

Garcia was a tall and solid man. An 1860 graduate of West Point, he was now thirty-eight years old. He had held brevet major's rank during the Civil War, but that rank had been reduced to lieutenant afterward. He had since received his permanent captaincy. Wounded and captured, he had spent the last part of the war at Andersonville.

He reached the ambulance, halted the team, and hurried to the rear. The bodies of the four troopers who had been escorting the colonel's wife were piled inside. The driver lay slumped across the others. There was no sign of Stephanie Detrick.

A sudden hollowness came to Garcia's chest. Stephanie Detrick gone meant that she was either dead or, more likely, a prisoner. Apaches had attacked the ambulance, killed the men escorting it, and taken her.

He heard running footsteps and turned his head. Colonel Detrick was a thick-bodied man of fifty. His round face never seemed to tan. It only got redder when he was exposed to the sun. He was out of breath and there was a look that was almost panic in his eyes. He said, "Stephanie?" making the word a question, which Garcia answered with a reluctant shake of his head.

Detrick reached the ambulance. He stared into the rear, his face turning gray. He breathed, "Oh God! Oh my God!"

Troopers streamed toward the halted ambulance. Standing at the rear of the rig, Garcia suddenly noticed that the driver was breathing. Shallowly, but breathing.

He bawled, "Stretcher! Quickly!"

Detrick crowded close. Garcia said, "Private Roark is alive."

A couple of troopers came running with a stretcher. Garcia supervised the lifting of Roark out of the ambulance. Roark was carried away. Garcia ordered several troopers to lift out the other men and he examined each carefully for signs of life. He found none.

Detrick stood by, numb and stunned. Finally he raised his glance and stared at Garcia. "I want to see you in my quarters, Captain," he said in a voice that shook.

"Yes, sir." Garcia watched him walk away. He didn't know how Detrick had risen to the rank of colonel and to the command of this isolated post. But he had to admit to himself that his opinion might be colored by the fact that Detrick was the one who had married Stephanie while he himself was rotting in Andersonville. He had been engaged to marry her himself when the war broke out. Confined at Andersonville for sixteen months, he had been given up for dead and he supposed he couldn't blame her for marrying. But it wasn't surprising that he didn't like the man who had married her.

He turned his head. To Corporal Delaney he said, "Load the bodies back into the ambulance. Take them to the hospital. Tell the surgeon to get them ready for burial tomorrow."

"Yes, sir." Corporal Delaney turned and began directing the reloading of the four bodies into the ambulance.

Garcia watched. He tried not to think of Stephanie in the Apaches' hands. How they treated her depended, he knew, on why they had captured her.

What he had to find out now was where the attack had taken place, how many savages had participated in it, and whether Stephanie had really been kidnapped or whether she had been killed.

He turned and headed across the parade toward officers' row on the far side of it.

Fort Lincoln, Arizona Territory, bore little resemblance to the traditional concept of a frontier fort. There was no stockade as such, only a fence around the stable area made of twisted, spindly poles, their thick ends buried in a trench. Frontier duty here was different than it was up north where there was danger of mass Indian attack. There were fewer Indians and they were scattered over a much larger area. Furthermore, the Apache style of fighting was different. They were hit-and-run fighters, never meeting the army head on unless they had been cornered and had no other choice.

A long gallery fronted the row of adobe officers' quarters. Colonel Detrick's quarters were in the center, next to Headquarters. Garcia knocked on the door, entered when he heard Detrick call, "Come in, Captain."

He stepped inside. It was dusk now, all the rose-golden

glow having faded from the western sky. An orderly was busy lighting lamps. Detrick looked at the orderly and said, "You may go."

"Yes, sir." The man glanced at Garcia, then turned and went out the door, closing it behind him.

Detrick paced nervously back and forth. His eyes were narrowed as if he was in pain and his face was pale. He was chewing on a dead cigar. Suddenly and explosively, he said, "Damn it, if it wasn't for you, she'd never have insisted on coming here!"

"Colonel, I had nothing to do with it."

"I suppose you are going to tell me you have not been corresponding with her."

"That's exactly what I'm telling you," Garcia said stiffly. "I doubt if she even knew that I was here."

"Oh she knew all right. That's why she was so damned anxious to come."

Garcia stared at Detrick unbelievingly. "Is that what *she* said?"

"No, it is not what she said. What she said was that she was tired of us living separately. I told her not to come, but she came anyway."

Garcia did not reply, because he had a feeling that Detrick would dispute anything he said.

There was a knock on the door. Detrick, red with the anger he was having trouble suppressing, called harshly, "Who is it?"

"Hiram Shaver, Colonel."

"Well, come in."

The door opened and a civilian came in. He was a scrawny, dried-up man with a skin as dark as any Indian's. Blue eyes made a startling contrast to the color of his skin.

Shaver was the civilian scout employed by Colonel Detrick. He was an unsmiling, taciturn man who enjoyed camaraderie neither with officers nor with enlisted men. A loner, he kept to himself and, while he was generally disliked, nobody could question his knowledge of the enemy. It was said he had an Apache wife and a couple of half-breed kids someplace. Shaver said, "Figured you'd want me, Colonel." He let his pale blue eyes rest appraisingly on Detrick a moment, then shifted his glance to Garcia. There was a subtle change in their expression when he did.

Detrick said, "I do, Shaver. Since Mrs. Detrick's body was not with the others I think we have to assume they've kidnapped her. I want you to tell me what they'll do to her. Will they . . . ?" He didn't seem able to put this fear into words.

But Shaver understood. "Depends, Colonel. If they intended killin' her they'd likely have left her dead right where they took her after makin' her die as slow as possible and havin' their pleasure with her while she was doin' it."

Detrick's face grew darker red. Garcia felt a stab of irritation within himself at the way Shaver was twisting the knife in Detrick, who was already beside himself with worry for his wife.

Shaver was carefully studying the faces of the two officers, apparently aware that the two had been arguing. He went on, "If there was some other reason for takin' her, then they likely won't hurt her much. For now at least. They'll make her work and they might beat her, but otherwise she won't be hurt."

Garcia asked, "What other reason could there be?"

Shaver put his pale blue, nearly expressionless eyes on the captain. He said, "I know Apaches, Captain, but nobody reads their minds. Maybe one of them wanted her for his squaw."

Garcia said, "Colonel, I think we ought to talk to Roark."

Detrick nodded. "All right. Go over there and wait. As soon as he comes to, send for me."

"Yes, sir." Garcia hesitated. "Will you be putting a force into the field tomorrow?"

"Of course I will. How big a force will depend on what Roark has to say."

Garcia nodded. He went to the door and opened it. He glanced at Shaver as he went out. Shaver's expressions were not easily read, but Garcia could have sworn he saw satisfaction in the scout's face.

He closed the door, leaving Shaver with the colonel. As he walked away along the gallery in the deepening dusk, he could hear their voices behind him, the words indistinguishable.

The day had been a hot one and even with the sun down it still was hot. A small breeze stirred, evaporating the sweat that had soaked his shirt and cooling him slightly in spite of the heat.

He forced himself not to think of Stephanie, uncomfortably aware that he had been thinking about her far too much in the past few weeks since he had first learned she was on her way. She was Detrick's wife and that was that. It was a thing that could not be changed.

But remembering her and thinking of her in the hands of the cruel Apaches was intolerable. He cursed softly beneath his breath, fished a cigar from his pocket, paused and lighted it. It was a strong, twisted Mexican cigar but it had a calming effect on his thoughts.

He reached the hospital and went inside. He could smell iodoform and formaldehyde and several other odors he could not identify. There was a small office here, the surgeon's, and a door that led to a ward with six beds in it. He opened it and stepped into the ward, where an orderly was busy lighting lamps.

Private Roark lay on the cot nearest the door. Four of the other five cots were occupied by the bodies of the dead troopers, with blankets pulled over their faces. The surgeon, Asa Gilpatrick, stood looking down at Roark, who now had a bandage around his head.

Garcia asked, "How is he?"

"Blow on the head. Concussion, I think. Possibly a fractured skull."

"No other wounds?"

The surgeon shook his head.

"Then they must not have intended killing him."

Gilpatrick, short, paunchy, and fifty, shrugged.

"How long before he can talk?"

"I might be able to bring him out of it."

"Do that. It's important that I talk to him."

Gilpatrick got a small bottle, uncorked it, and held it under Trooper Roark's nose. The man coughed and turned his head. Gilpatrick followed his nose with the bottle. Roark coughed again and opened his eyes.

The colonel had said he wanted to be called as soon as Roark was able to talk. Garcia glanced at the hospital orderly. "Go tell the colonel that Roark is awake."

The man went out. Garcia asked, "What happened, Roark? How many of them were there?"

"The colonel's lady. They took her, sir."

There was fear in Roark's eyes. Garcia said sternly, "I know, Roark. How many of them were there?"

Roark moved his head slightly and winced. He said, "I

didn't count, but there were a lot. Maybe twenty or twenty-five. They took us by surprise."

"Did you load the bodies?"

"Yes, sir. I got started back and then passed out."

The colonel came in, followed by the orderly. He said harshly, "What happened, Private? Did they kill my wife or did they take her prisoner?"

Roark shook his head. "They didn't kill her, sir. At least I didn't find her when I came to."

"Did you even look for her?" There was unreasoning anger in the colonel's voice.

"Well, I looked around where the bodies of the men were." Roark seemed to wince under the impact of the colonel's glare. "I didn't follow the Indians, sir. I . . . I guess I just figured they had taken her."

Detrick started to say something, then changed his mind.

Garcia said, "Roark said twenty or twenty-five. That's a lot of Indians for a hunting or raiding party. Maybe they knew your wife was coming and were waiting there for her."

"How the hell could they know that? They must have just happened on the ambulance, seen there was a woman inside, and decided to kidnap her."

Garcia didn't dispute the colonel's statement. But neither was he convinced. The very size of the attacking party tended to rule out the colonel's theory.

# CHAPTER 3

Stephanie Detrick was a good horsewoman. She was not used to riding astride but doing so presented no difficulty.

Her hat, which would have shaded her head and her face, had been left behind in the ambulance. Now the sun beat mercilessly down on her. She had thought it hot before but the direct heat of the sun was almost unbearable. While her body perspired profusely, the skin on her face, neck, and hands seemed to shrink as it dried and burned in the blistering rays of the afternoon sun.

She knew, at first, a feeling of bleak despair. The Indians had killed the four members of the escort and, as far as she knew, the driver too. Word of what had happened might not reach her husband for days. By that time she might be many miles away.

She had heard her share of tales of what the Indians did to white women they captured. Now, as she thought about it, terror came over her. Her body, even in the awful heat, chilled. Her knees trembled and she gripped the horse with them so that her captors wouldn't see. She clenched her hands in an effort to keep them from trembling.

Covertly she glanced up at the Indians riding in front of her. None seemed to be paying any attention to her. A faint flicker of hope touched her thoughts. If they intended to abuse her, why had they not done so already? Why take her with them if they meant to abuse and kill her anyway?

The hope died when she thought they might have taken her because they wanted to take their time with her. Tonight when they made camp.

At that thought, her whole body began to shake. Her teeth chattered. Angrily she fought herself for control. This was what they wanted. They wanted her to be terrified. And she wasn't going to give them the satisfaction. She was their prisoner and what they wanted to do to her they'd do, no matter what she felt or did or didn't do. She had just as well accept the fact of her own complete helplessness. She had no weapon and little chance of getting one.

Once she accepted her own helplessness, she stopped shaking so violently. God's will would be done. If she was to die at the hands of these savages then it would be because her time had come to die.

She could not convince herself that coming here had been wrong. She had wanted a complete marriage, not one where she and her husband lived a thousand miles apart. She knew well enough why he wanted to live separately from her, but she saw no reason why that could not be changed, not if both of them worked at it. There was nothing physically wrong with Hans Detrick. She was sure of that.

There was only one thing wrong with all of her self-justification, and she guiltily admitted it. She had known all the time that Logan Garcia was there. If she was going to be honest with herself she was going to have to admit that she had felt excited at the thought of seeing him again. Not that anything could possibly come of it. She was married to Hans Detrick and that was that. Divorce would be unthinkable. It would ruin her husband's career and Garcia's too.

The Apaches' horses plodded steadily through the barren scattering of cactus and rock, skirting even more barren mountains, descending into dry washes and climbing out again. She thought of the troopers and the ambulance driver lying dead back there in the sun. If it was not for her, they would not have died. They would not have been in this place at this time and they would still be alive. Coming here might not, in itself, have been wrong. But her coming had already cost five lives and the more she thought about it, the stronger was her guilty certainty that it was going to cost more. Colonel Detrick would eventually discover that the Apaches had taken her. He would try to find her, making war on the Indians in the attempt. Indians would die. So would troopers under her husband's command.

Unwillingly, she remembered each of the escort troopers. She had gotten to know them all during the trip from Lordsburg. One, Corporal Benjamin, had had a wife and child. She closed her eyes and tears squeezed out between her tight-closed lids.

The horse she was riding wore a McClellan saddle and she shifted her position often to ease the places it chafed. The sun began slowly to descend toward the horizon ahead of them.

Trying to take her mind off her terror-filled thoughts, she counted the Apaches ahead of her. There were nine. At a place where the trail bent sharply, she glanced behind, counting those following her. There were twelve.

All were villainous looking as far as she was concerned. Nearly naked, each wore only a scanty breechclout secured by a belt around his waist. Headbands kept their coarse black hair out of their eyes. They wore high-topped leather moccasins on their feet.

Some of their horses had saddles, scanty affairs covered and sewn with rawhide. The others rode bareback, although some of them had blankets thrown over their horses' backs.

Rifles were slung across the backs of about half of them,

and some had leather bandoliers of cartridges slung diagonally the opposite way. Those who did not have rifles had short bows, strung with sinew, and rawhide quivers containing feathered arrows. At the waist of each man was a knife in a leather sheath. There was scanty beadwork on a few of these.

Many of their horses wore brands on their hips and, since Stephanie knew enough about Indians to know they did not usually brand their animals, she assumed these horses had been stolen from the whites. Probably after those whites had been murdered, she thought bleakly.

Stephanie Detrick was no different from most other white people of the period. She believed that the Indians were closely akin to the other savage animals that inhabited the wild regions of the western territories. She gave them credit for little intelligence and for no civilization. They constituted a barrier to settlement. They murdered white settlers and travelers. Her husband and others like him were here to contain, or exterminate, the Indians. The way she felt right now, she wished extermination had been completed a long time ago.

She discovered it helped if she hated the Indians. It made her feel less terrified. So she nurtured her hatred and fed it with her thoughts.

The afternoon dragged to a close. The Indians seemed to be in no hurry. Nor did they seem to be making any effort to hide their trail. Once, looking back, she could see that their horses' hoofprints made a trail as wide almost as a road and as plain. Obviously either they did not fear the soldiers or they wanted to be followed.

That twenty-one Apaches would not fear several times their number was inconceivable. Therefore, they must want to be followed and that meant there were more Apaches somewhere ahead. The appalling thought struck her that she was being used as bait—to draw the troops away from Fort Lincoln so that they could be ambushed by a larger number of Indians.

The sun dropped below the horizon. The Indians halted in a shallow draw. There were a few trees growing at the side of the narrow, dry watercourse. Several of the Indians dug holes in the sand with their hands. Water seeped in to fill the holes to a level about a foot below the surface. They watered their horses first, then unsaddled and released them, except for one. The horses stayed within a hundred yards of camp, browsing the few scrubby trees that grew along the dry stream bed.

Stephanie didn't know what to do. One of the Indians, dark-faced, with pockmarks hardly improving his ugly and menacing appearance, approached and spoke to her in rapid Apache. She did not understand and looked at him blankly. He spoke to her in Spanish, but she understood this no better. He scowled at her a moment and then knocked her down.

Her mouth bleeding, she struggled to her feet. Her eyes were blazing with anger. The Apache struck her again, but this time it was not so unexpected and she managed to keep her feet.

Her eyes were virulent. He laughed in her face. She braced herself for another blow, but instead, he picked up a dry stick from the ground, then gestured away from camp. They wanted her to gather wood, she realized. Still glaring, she nodded her head and turned her back on the Indian. She wandered away, picking up wood as she went. When she had an armload, she returned to camp with it. She dumped it on the ground and went back for more.

The thought occurred to her that she could keep going if

she wished. They weren't watching her. If she could keep from being caught until dark, she might get away in the darkness.

She discarded the idea almost as quickly as she had it. She was no match for a score of Apache Indians. They'd let her go all night, wearing herself out in flight. Then they'd calmly trail her in the morning and would probably beat her insensible when they caught up with her.

She returned with a second load of wood and went after a third. She was weary and weak from heat and fear, but she worked steadily. So far, she thought, no one had even looked at her as if they meant her any harm. They were treating her exactly, she supposed, as they would have treated one of their own squaws. Which probably meant that she was safe, for the time being at least. They did not intend to rape or torture her. They did not intend to kill her either. She apparently had greater value to them alive and unhurt than dead.

She kept going, despite her weariness, until one of the Apaches signaled her to stop. He beckoned and, trembling inwardly, she went to him. He handed her some of the same kind of reddish-black dried meat upon which the Indians were chewing. He offered her his skin canteen and she took it and drank deeply before giving it back. The water had a brackish taste as well as a taste given it by the receptacle in which it had been kept, but she was thirsty and to her it tasted good. After she handed back the canteen the Apache didn't even look at her. She sat down at the base of a scrubby tree with her back to it and tried to gnaw a piece off the tough dried meat. This was what they called jerky, she supposed, and there was probably a lot of nourishment in it.

She was surprised to find that it was tasty once you got it softened up a bit by chewing it.

She finished the jerky. The Apaches sat around the fire for a while, but not for long. One by one, they stretched themselves out on the ground, like dogs lying down to sleep, with no ceremony, no blankets, no conversation with their fellows.

She stretched out herself, after hollowing out a depression for her hip, the way some of the Apaches had done. She closed her eyes.

The future stretched bleakly away in front of her. By now she was convinced that she was the bait for a trap they meant to set for her husband and his troops. The trap was going to work, too. Pride wouldn't let Colonel Hans Detrick permit his wife to remain a captive without making some kind of effort to rescue her.

Being only bait, she knew she was expendable. Once they'd lured the white soldiers into a trap, the Apaches would have no further use for her. They'd probably kill her as soon as the battle began.

Stephanie Detrick was a sensible woman. She knew there was nothing she could do right now to change her predicament. But that didn't mean something would not turn up.

In the meantime it was going to be a lot easier on her if she did what the Apaches told her to. Dutifully and silently and without resentment the way one of their squaws would have behaved.

Hard work wasn't going to hurt her. Her feet might get raw and so might her hands. The sun would bleach and dry her hair, burn and blister her face, neck, and hands. But she was going to survive. When her husband and Logan Garcia came for her, she was going to be alive.

# CHAPTER 4

Fort Lincoln sat on the north bank of Chiricahua Creek about five miles from the place where it came running clear out of the barren hills. Back in the hills there were a few scrubby cottonwoods and willows along its banks, and these extended for a short way out onto the plain, but where the fort stood there were none.

Those who had built the fort here had planned it well. A log dam a mile upstream raised the water level enough so that it could be channeled into ditches to both the north and south of the creek. The ditches irrigated the native grass sufficiently to grow hay, a necessity if cavalry were to be stationed here. Grain could be freighted in. Hay could not.

The hay had been stacked close in, to make it defensible in case of an Indian attack, and fenced. After each cutting, the horses were pastured on the stubble under guard until the new growth began to come on.

There was not always a surface flow in Chiricahua Creek, but there was always an underground flow sufficient for the needs of the fort. A well and windmill stood on the bank of the creek, with a large storage tank at the windmill's base from which the fort's water was drawn.

Fuel for cooking was brought in regularly by a wood-cutting detail which went out into the hills and cut cedars and ironwood. Both burned with a hot and steady flame.

Sergeant Timothy Hazelthorne was a grizzled veteran of twenty-two years' service, much of it spent in places like this, frontier outposts in a barren and hostile land. He had fought the Apaches many times and had profound respect for their courage, cunning, and ability to survive in this hostile environment.

Respect did not imply liking, however. Tim Hazelthorne hated the savages as he had never hated anything else in his life. He had gathered up the remains of too many innocent white settlers and travelers for burial to feel anything but hatred for those who had perpetrated the crimes.

He was waiting for Captain Garcia when the captain reached his quarters. Garcia said, "Come in, Sergeant."

Hazelthorne followed him into the barren, adobe-walled room that served as Garcia's quarters. The floor was bare and there were cracks between the rough-sawed boards. Paths of smoothness had been worn between the door, the bed, and the dresser, upon which were a pitcher and washpan and above which hung a mirror. Garcia gestured toward one of the two chairs. "Sit down, Sergeant."

"Yes, sir." Hazelthorne had removed his hat. He had a shock of coarse red hair, plastered down with sweat where the hatband had been. His face was leathery, dark, but burned across the nose by the sun in spite of his years of exposure to it. He sat on the edge of the straight-backed chair and began rotating his hat in his hands.

Garcia said, "We'll be going after them first thing in the morning. Get the troop ready. I've got a hunch we'll be out for a while."

"The men will be ready, sir," Hazelthorne said and Garcia knew they would.

He was silent a moment and then he asked, "How well do you know Hiram Shaver?"

Hazelthorne shot him a quick and puzzled glance. He shrugged. "Nobody knows that one, sir."

"How long has he been at Lincoln?"

"Close to two years, sir. Came here after Jake Reese was killed."

"What happened to Reese?"

"He got careless I guess. Apaches caught him and staked him out in the sun with a strip of rawhide around his head. Time he was found, the rawhide had just about buried itself in his flesh." His eyes met Garcia's and there was a mute kind of anguish in them. He said, "I never seen such an expression on a human face. It was a look of pure agony." He shook himself visibly as if he could shake off the memory.

"Got careless? Isn't that a little strange? An experienced scout like Reese getting careless enough to get caught?"

"Wasn't like him, if that's what you mean. Jake wasn't the kind to get careless when there was hostiles around."

"And that's when Shaver came to this post? To replace Reese?"

"Yes, sir. Shaver came from Fort Apache. Happened they could spare him."

"Is Shaver married?"

Hazelthorne hesitated, then said, "If you call havin' a squaw a marriage, then I guess he is. Or at least he used to be when I was stationed at Fort Apache."

"When was that?"

"Three years ago."

"Does he have any kids?"

"Two. Both boys. I never saw 'em, though, or the squaw either, for that matter. They never came to the post. He kep' 'em out in the Indian village in a wickiup."

Garcia was frowning. He studied his sergeant closely for a moment. There was a hidden look of worry in Hazelthorne's face that Garcia, who knew him very well, could see no matter how carefully Hazelthorne tried to keep it hidden. He could also guess its cause. Hazelthorne's wife, Lela, was here at Fort Lincoln. She did laundry for the officers and she had a bold way of looking at a man that didn't become a respectable wife. Hazelthorne was afraid, and probably rightly so, that she'd be taking up with someone before he'd been gone twenty-four hours from the post.

Hazelthorne asked, "Is that all, Captain?"

Garcia nodded. "Yes."

"Yes, sir." Hazelthorne went out, closing the door behind him.

Garcia tilted the chair back against the adobe wall of his room and stared at the whitewashed pole rafters of the ceiling. Despite the thick adobe walls of the building and the thick brush-and-sod roof, the room was like an oven. He got up, crossed to the window and opened it. There was no breeze as yet and it felt no better with the window open than it had with the window shut.

He thought of Stephanie in the hands of the Indians. If he was right, if they had seized her as a hostage, they would not kill her. But they would make living a veritable hell for her. She would be treated like a slave, which now she was and which she would remain unless they found and rescued her.

Beautiful as she was, fragile as she seemed, Garcia knew she was much less helpless than she appeared. Stephanie Detrick was a strong woman and she would take a lot before she broke.

He also knew that, tough as she might be, she would not be able to take what she was going to have to take in the next few days or weeks. There probably wasn't a white woman alive who could. Stephanie might be tough enough mentally but physically she was not—not for the terrible heat, the pace of travel, the lack of food and water, and the endless riding from dawn to dusk. To say nothing of the hard physical work that would be required of her when they were not traveling.

He sat down again, tilted back the chair and closed his eyes. He tried to remember what she had looked like but it had been too long. He could not bring her image into his mind, however hard he tried.

He had loved her once, deeply and strongly. He had asked her to marry him. She was probably the reason he hadn't married since.

He could remember the horror that had been Andersonville and sometimes he had thought the only thing that kept him fighting to stay alive had been the promise of going back to Stephanie.

He got up impatiently and began to pace back and forth. Stephanie was the colonel's wife and forever beyond his reach. He was a fool to think about her.

He went out onto the gallery and felt the breeze begin to stir in the west. He heard the sounds of the post. A shrill whinnying came from a couple of horses briefly skirmishing down at the stables. He heard a man shout, and he heard one of the laundresses shrilly scolding one of her children. A dog barked, and from the sutler's store at the end of officers' row came the sounds of men laughing.

Garcia thought that, like most of the other officers, he ought to hate his duty here. But he did not. He loved the barren reach of desert. He loved the pastels of lavender and rose that stained the distant rocky peaks at sundown and at sunrise again.

He even loved the heat and he realized with some surprise that he was looking forward to the campaign that would begin tomorrow. Fighting was a soldier's job and Garcia was a professional.

Like Garcia, Tim Hazelthorne was a professional. He also was looking forward to the campaign that would begin tomorrow. Fighting was what a soldier was for.

But as he left Captain Garcia's quarters, he was frowning worriedly. He wanted to go, but he hated the thought of leaving his wife alone here at the post.

Angrily he shook his head. He shouldn't care what she did. He ought to have better sense. She would take up with anyone wearing pants. He knew her for what she was and he shouldn't care what she did. Not anymore.

The trouble was, he did care. For two very valid reasons. One was that, he was still in love with her and couldn't help being jealous of her. The second was that every time she rolled in the hay with someone else it managed to get around all over the post, even to the other troops. And he knew the men sniggered behind his back because he couldn't hold on to his own wife. Or pitied him, which was worse.

C Troop's barracks was one of four large adobe buildings on the opposite side of the parade. By the time he reached it, the sky was almost completely dark and a few stars were winking out.

Sergeant Hazelthorne spoke to the men lounging outside in the cooling night air. "Come on inside."

Inside, he shouted, "Pay attention now. Reveille will be at four. We move out at six. Any man who isn't ready and whose horse isn't ready will get thirty days in the stockade."

There was an immediate buzz of talk. Hazelthorne turned on his heel and went out. He strode along the covered gallery toward the NCO quarters at the end of the row of barracks buildings.

His wife was lounging against one of the poles that supported the gallery. The top three buttons of her blouse were gone and her thin cotton skirt clung to her, stuck to her body by perspiration. Light from the open doorway behind her illuminated her and cast her shadow on the bare ground at the edge of the gallery.

Men in front of the nearest barracks, that of K Troop, were watching her and she knew it. There was a half smile on her mouth.

Hazelthorne clenched his jaws. He said, "I suppose you've heard about the colonel's wife."

She said, "I heard."

He wanted to hit her for flaunting herself so openly. He knew she was doing it deliberately, letting him see it deliberately. He said, "Three troops will be going out at dawn."

"Which troops?"

He said, "B, C, and K," wondering even as he spoke how a man could simultaneously want to hit a woman and make love to her.

"How long will you be gone?" The question was innocent enough of itself, a normal question, but the inflection in her voice was not. It was as if she was thinking only of the freedom she would have during the time he was away.

"She don't give a damn," he thought, "what happens to me." He took a step toward her, his face coming into the light streaming out of the open door.

The taunting look faded from her face. For just an instant he saw fear in her eyes and then it was gone as quickly as it had appeared. He had been married to her for seven years and he'd never laid a hand on her. She knew he wasn't going to now.

He went inside, got a brown bottle from the shelf, and poured himself a drink. She came in and stood looking at him, legs spread, hands on hips. "So the Indians got the colonel's fancy wife." Hazelthorne could tell she was thinking about what the savages would do to the colonel's wife. And relishing it, because the repeated rape of the colonel's wife brought her down from her haughty place in life.

Hazelthorne said, "Maybe they'll come get you while we're gone. There's only going to be one troop left behind." He stared at her, his eyes suddenly hard. "You'd like that, wouldn't you? Maybe for once in your life you'd get all the men you want."

She laughed. But the laugh was forced and she didn't meet his glance.

Hazelthorne gulped the fiery Mexican liquor and poured himself some more. Lela went into the tiny kitchen and began rattling pots and pans. Hazelthorne stared moodily out the open door. A fly buzzed around his head, finally landing on his ear. He batted at it savagely.

Getting up suddenly, he corked the bottle and returned it to the cupboard. He went out into the darkness and strode briskly across the parade. A bugler blew mess call. A dog barked at the sound of a coyote yelping out on the desert. The night and the night sounds around him were familiar and the scowl gradually faded from Tim Hazelthorne's face.

# CHAPTER 5

Hiram Shaver left the colonel's quarters as mess call sounded across the parade. He paused long enough on the gallery to pack and light a stubby pipe. His face, in the glow of the match, was dark and saturnine, his eyes glittering and unreadable. If a man had been asked to characterize his expression he probably would have said satanic.

Taciturnity of outward expression hid what went on inside Hiram Shaver's mind. He felt elation now. The initial step of his plan had worked with precision. The Apaches had Colonel Detrick's wife. They had accomplished the kidnapping without the loss of a single man.

Tomorrow he would lead Detrick and three troops out of Fort Lincoln. They would go to the place where the attack on the ambulance had taken place. They would follow the trail left by the hostiles, which would lead them to the abandoned site of a large village. They would then continue to follow the kidnappers of the colonel's wife, ignoring all the other trails.

Day after day the blistering heat of the desert would wear down both men and animals. They would find water only when the Apaches deemed it essential to keep them from turning back. And then, when they were completely exhausted, they would suddenly find their prey, reinforced now by all the men who had been in the village. Manuelito, the Apache chief, could put two hundred fighters into the field and would make short work of the exhausted troops. Particularly since he meant to ambush them.

That was the plan. It had evolved over a period of more than two years, ever since a patrol under Colonel Detrick had come upon and attacked a small Apache village. A few had escaped but the wife of Hiram Shaver had been killed, as had his two half-breed sons.

One of the survivors had brought the word to Shaver at Fort Apache. He rode immediately to the burned-out village. He talked to the survivors who had buried the dead and from them he satisfied himself that neither his wife nor his sons had managed to escape.

Squaw man he might be called among the whites and it was true that he and his Indian wife had not been married according to the white man's law. But he had loved her deeply and his two sons had given his life a richness and meaning he had not previously thought possible.

The village where Shaver's wife and sons were living had been a peaceful one despite the fact that its occupants were off the reservation. The attack was unwarranted and unjustified. Detrick had made the attack for the sole purpose of giving those of his men who were green a taste of action. It was a random attack, with no more meaning for the colonel than an order for an inspection of quarters or a close-order drill.

Shaver went back to Fort Apache, suddenly changed from the easygoing, if tough, solitude-loving man he had been. He became brooding and morose. He drove what few friends he had had away from him with his snarling surliness.

And frustration made him even more surly and morose. He wanted vengeance against Colonel Detrick and his troops. But how was he to obtain it when Detrick was a hundred miles away?

Getting himself assigned to Fort Lincoln became an absolute necessity. So he got a leave, rode south to Fort Lincoln, and waited there, mostly within sight of the fort, for three weeks before Jake Reese ventured forth on one of his periodic scouts of the vicinity.

Hiram Shaver liked Jake Reese. Or he had until Reese led Colonel Detrick and his troops to the village where Shaver's wife and sons were living. Now, it was different. He hated Reese as much as he hated Colonel Detrick, because he figured Reese could have stopped the attack if he'd wanted to.

He waited until Reese was several miles from the fort. Then he stepped out from behind a rock and confronted him. Reese was surprised but not afraid. Shaver said, "Getting careless, Jake. It'll be the death of you."

Reese agreed ruefully. "I guess I'm getting old." He dismounted and fished a Bull Durham sack and papers from the pocket of his shirt. He made one for himself, then handed the sack to Shaver.

Shaver took it with his left hand, then hit Reese on the side of the head with a rock he was holding in his right. The man fell, scattering flake tobacco on the ground as he did.

When he awoke, his hands were tied and so were his feet. He was lying face up in the sun, which was directly overhead. He turned his head and saw Shaver sitting on a rock a dozen feet away, smoking a Bull Durham cigarette. He said plaintively, "What the hell did you do that for?"

The words were hardly out of his mouth before he felt the strip of rawhide Shaver had tied around his head. He understood immediately what Shaver was doing to him but he still didn't know the reason for it. Feeling how tight the rawhide strip already was, he asked again, "Why? What the hell did I ever do to you?"

Shaver stared at him without answering for a long time, while the rawhide strip got tighter and tighter. Reese's head had already begun to ache but he knew it was nothing compared to the way it would ache before he died. Finally Shaver said, "You remember that little Apache village you led the colonel to a couple of months ago?"

"At Arroyo Blanco? Sure. I remember, but I didn't lead him there. We just happened onto it."

Shaver said, "You knew I had an Indian wife, didn't you? Well, she was in that village on Arroyo Blanco and so were my two boys. All three of them were killed so that goddamn colonel could give his green troopers a little battle practice. Not that it was much of a battle."

Reese now knew there was no use trying to talk his way out of this. There was no use telling Shaver that he'd tried to persuade the colonel to let the little Indian village alone. And there was no use pleading for his life. He could tell that by looking at the stone-hard set of Shaver's face.

He thought about how tight that strip of rawhide was going to get before death mercifully rescued him. He said, "You and me go back a long ways. I don't reckon you're goin' to let me live but seems like you'd make it quick, for old times' sake."

He knew before the words were out of his mouth that he was wasting his breath. This man was not the Hiram Shaver he had known. Shaver's face was as implacable as that of any Apache. The truth was, Shaver was probably more Apache now than he was white.

Reese closed his eyes. He clenched his fists behind his back. He forced himself to go back over his life, because thinking of something else was the only way he was going to be able to endure the rapidly increasing pain in his head.

He had wanted to come west for as long as he could remember, so he had run away from home at fourteen. He'd talked himself into a fur expedition setting out from St. Louis for the upper reaches of the Missouri.

He hadn't been home since. He seldom even thought about home. And he'd never written to his parents, because he figured they were mad at him for running away when he was needed so much at home.

This was how it was going to end. Tied, staked out in the blistering desert sun to die from a shrinking rawhide thong tied around his head.

The pain was now so intense that he could hardly think of anything else. His eyes were closed tightly because even the sun, seeping through their lids, caused the pain to increase. He turned his head so that he might get some relief from the glare.

He tried to remember all the women he had bedded with in his life. Going back from now, he tried to count them and remember what they had looked like.

He heard someone groaning and did not realize that the sounds came from his own mouth. Finally he heard a man screaming and he still did not know the screaming came from his own lips. His face was twisted into an expression of pure agony. Hiram Shaver sat on the rock and rolled himself another cigarette with Reese's tobacco. His face showed no expression of any kind. It was as if he was alone.

The time inevitably came when Jake Reese could no longer think. And at last he mercifully lost consciousness.

Shaver stayed until his chest had stopped its rise and fall. Then, calmly, he went to where he had left his horse. He mounted and rode north to Fort Apache. The commandant at Fort Lincoln would ask the commandant at Apache for a replacement. Shaver knew he would be sent because he had become the least liked of the three scouts regularly employed there.

And he *was* sent to Fort Lincoln. The impending arrival of the colonel's wife had given him the chance he had waited so long and so patiently for.

Vengeance now was very near. Tomorrow he would lead Detrick's troopers out into the desert after the hostiles that had kidnapped the colonel's wife. Manuelito would do his part and Shaver would do his. Not a man of the three troops would ever get back alive.

He crossed the parade to the mess hall, which was already full. He got in line, was served, and went to a table where he could sit by himself. Not one of the troopers present sat with him.

He smiled sourly to himself. He didn't want their company, so if they thought they were hurting him with their ostracism they were mistaken.

But he knew very well why they avoided him. They sensed the bitter hatred toward them that was in his heart.

Finished with his eating, he got up and went outside. The night was hardly cooler than the day had been. He packed and lighted his stubby pipe, then headed for the stables.

Shaver had three horses of his own. He looked each of them over carefully, lifting each of their four feet and studying them in lantern light. He selected a chunky sorrel as the horse he would ride tomorrow. The shoes on the sorrel were nearly new and he had the most stamina of the three.

Next he went to the sutler's store and bought a few of the things he knew he was going to need. Tobacco for his pipe. Sulphur matches. Some .44 caliber cartridges for his revolver. A plentiful supply of jerky that the sutler had bought from some friendly Indians and some hardtack biscuits. Carrying the supplies in a gunnysack, he headed for his quarters, one of the smaller rooms across the parade were the NCO quarters were.

For a time, he sat on the gallery staring out across the parade, listening to the familiar sounds. In a week, he would see his long-cherished obsession realized. He would be the only survivor of the force that rode out of Fort Lincoln tomorrow.

Or maybe he'd be killed. With his family gone, that didn't matter the way it would have once.

There were parallels in his life and that of Jake Reese, he thought. Like Reese, he had left home when very young. He had seen the land west of the Missouri when it was virgin and untouched. He had seen the land when native grass was higher than a horse's belly, and rippled in the wind like the waves of a golden sea. He had seen the great herds of buffalo—once nearly half a million animals in a single migrating herd that took a week to pass his camp.

When the demand for beaver was great, he had trapped. When the demand for Indian-made buffalo robes was great, he had traded with the Indians for them. Then, when there was demand for tough, huge buffalo hides, he had hunted buffalo, sometimes killing more than a hundred in a single day.

And finally when those things had gone, he had turned his knowledge of the land and the Indians into something he could make a living at. He had taken employment as an army scout.

Always, Shaver had been a solitary man. He liked being alone. Until seven years ago, casual contacts with women had been enough to satisfy the body hungers that torment a man. Then he had met the young Apache girl who became his wife. Afterward he spent at least a part of every year in the Apache village with her.

Two sons she bore him, the first after a year, the second two years after that.

Sitting there in the oppressive night heat, he remembered the two little boys. Scarcely lighter in color than full-blooded Apaches, they had been raised as Indians. The only difference was that Shaver had insisted that they learn English well.

Shaver had seen the settlement of the West. He had seen the way whites, one way or another, got the land away from the Indians. He knew the Indian way of life was doomed and he wanted his sons to be able to make their way in the white man's world.

Maybe, he thought, it was because he had been such a solitary man that his family had meant so much to him. To have them killed so a bunch of soldiers could have some shooting practice with little risk to themselves. . . . It had just been too much to bear.

# CHAPTER 6

Colonel Hans Detrick sat at his desk nearly motionless after Hiram Shaver left. He heard the faint sounds of the post, the voices of men at the sutler's store, the bark of a dog, the whinnying of a couple of horses in one of the corrals.

He had braced himself for Stephanie's arrival. The fact that she was not now coming left him feeling limp emotionally.

It didn't enter his head that there might have been a plan behind her kidnapping. He didn't give the Apaches credit for that much cunning and, besides, he thought, as many frontier officers did, that three or four troops of United States Cavalry could whip as many Indians as could be thrown against them. The times he had met and fought the Apaches reinforced that belief. They always ran away after exchanging a few shots with the troops.

He would lead his troops out tomorrow again. That was required of him, both by his orders as commandant of this post and by his instincts as a man. Pursuing the hostiles who had killed four of his men and kidnapped his wife was expected of him.

And pursue he would. Until he either had verified Stephanie's death or had rescued her.

He considered the latter eventuality remote. He believed that Stephanie either was dead or soon would be dead. Perhaps even now the Apaches were taking their pleasure with her and would leave her behind at the site of their first night's camp.

Detrick examined his own feelings critically. He was not a cold man, despite what Stephanie thought of him. Nor was he unfeeling. He regretted the fact that she had been captured by the Indians even though her capture had spared him much personal embarrassment. He didn't want her dead and he didn't want her suffering.

But he was also practical. Her capture *had* spared him much. If she was killed, he would never be forced to come face to face with his own inadequacy where she was concerned.

Nervously, he got out of his chair and began to pace back and forth. His orderly stuck his head in at the door to advise him that supper was being served in the officers' mess, and he directed the orderly to bring a tray to him here. The man withdrew.

Detrick resumed his pacing. How in the hell, he wondered, did a man get into a fix like the one he'd gotten himself into? He'd never been a womanizer, but neither had he been celibate. And until his wedding night with Stephanie, he'd thought of himself as a perfectly normal man.

His face burned as he remembered it. There was no getting around the facts, no matter how much he would like to. He had failed. He had failed and had run away, and with the memory of that failure in his mind he had never been able to succeed afterward. So he'd taken the only way out he could. He had gotten himself transferred and he'd left Stephanie behind. Why she hadn't divorced him, he didn't know. Perhaps her trip out here had been for the purpose of a showdown long delayed. She had probably meant to issue an ultimatum—either they would live together as man and wife, or she *would* get a divorce.

The orderly brought his supper and put it on the desk for him. Detrick sat down to eat, not so much because he was hungry as because it gave him something to do. But his mind remained active, so much so that later he couldn't even have said what it was he ate.

He thought of Logan Garcia, who had been engaged to Stephanie when the war broke out. He knew very well that she'd never have married him if Garcia hadn't been reported killed. He finished eating, got up, and began nervously to pace again.

After a while the orderly came for the tray and took it out. Detrick stepped out onto the gallery and lighted a cigar. He realized suddenly and with some surprise that he hated Logan Garcia. He hated the captain's calm self-assurance. He hated him because he suspected that Garcia would never fail as he had failed.

He hated Garcia even more because every time he looked at him, Garcia reminded him of his own failure, of his inadequacy as a man.

In the eleven years since his marriage to Stephanie, Detrick had only tried once with another woman, a prostitute. And, probably because he was so afraid, he had also failed with her. He could still hear her mocking laughter as he rushed away from the place.

Savagely he cursed beneath his breath. Only when Stephanie was dead could he be free, he thought. No. Not just Stephanie. Stephanie *and* Garcia. Then maybe he could forget. Then maybe he could overcome his fear of failure and then maybe he could begin to function as a man again.

Critically he turned his thoughts inward and examined his own mind. How much did he want Stephanie dead? Enough to make sure she was killed by the Indians before they could rescue her? Enough to fire a bullet into her himself during the heat of battle if there was no other way?

He couldn't answer those questions honestly because he didn't know. Maybe he would try to ensure her death at the hands of the Indians. But he doubted if he could cold-bloodedly kill her himself.

And what about Captain Garcia? Hating the man, jealous of him, could he shoot Garcia during the battle? He didn't think he could but it would depend, he supposed, on what his state of mind was at the time.

There was considerable activity down at the stables as the men who were going tomorrow looked after their mounts. Both blacksmith forges were shooting sparks high into the air as horses that needed it were freshly shod.

Detrick went back into his room and closed the door. He got a brown bottle of whiskey out of a drawer and poured himself a drink. And another. And another still.

His head was whirling when, from across the parade, he heard shouted imprecations and the other sounds that accompany a fight. Uneasily aware that he had had too much to drink, he got to his feet and staggered to the door.

Enough time had passed to make the outside air cool by comparison with that inside his room. He stepped out onto the gallery and stared in the direction from which the sounds were coming.

A crowd had gathered over in front of the NCO quarters. The shouting continued. Through the circle of spectators, he could see glimpses of the struggling bodies of two fighting men.

Colonel Detrick was aware that quarrels were sometimes settled with fists down behind the stables but it was a quiet, unobtrusive thing he could ignore. This was something that could not be ignored.

He started across the parade at a trot, trying to keep from staggering and wishing he hadn't had so much to drink. Men were running from all directions, eager to see what was going on.

Detrick reached the ring of spectators. Shouting, "Make way," he pushed through and they gave ground as they realized who he was. Four or five deep they were, but he finally reached the inner circle and could see the combatants.

One was Timothy Hazelthorne, Garcia's sergeant. The other was Sergeant Ferguson, assigned to E, the troop that would be staying behind tomorrow. Beyond the two struggling men Detrick saw Lela Hazelthorne, watching breathlessly, lips parted, her eyes catching the glints of a lantern somebody was holding high.

Detrick didn't need to be told the cause of the fight. Lela Hazelthorne had to be its cause. The way she paraded herself before the woman-hungry men in this isolated outpost practically ensured that something like this would happen sooner or later. What surprised Detrick was that it hadn't happened before this.

The two men separated briefly, and circled. Hazelthorne swiped impatiently at blood that streamed from his nose. Ferguson had a trickle of it coming from the corner of his mouth. Detrick shouted, "Stop it!" just as Hazelthorne charged.

Ferguson was bowled back by the force of that charge, knocked into the ring of spectators, which was all that kept him on his feet. When they separated again, Hazelthorne was staggering backward, looking at a bleeding cut six inches long on his right forearm, and Ferguson had a knife.

It was a butcher knife, one of those used in the mess hall for slicing meat. Ferguson must have taken it from one of the spectators, or else it had been handed to him. He advanced with it, face twisted, eyes glittering. Detrick shouted again, "Stop it. Immediately, do you hear?"

Neither man appeared to have heard. Detrick could feel himself swaying and his head felt light as air. His vision blurred.

Ferguson rushed, slashing with the knife. Hazelthorne avoided being cut only by arching his body away from the slashing blade.

Detrick stood there woodenly, not knowing what to do. Shouting orders at the men to stop seemed to have no effect. Even if he had been cold sober, it was doubtful if he would have interposed his own body between the men. Tipsy as he now was, doing so would have been disastrous.

Once more he shouted ineffectually, "Stop fighting, do you hear? That is an order!"

Ferguson rushed again. This time, Hazelthorne closed with him, managing to get the wrist of Ferguson's right hand in the grasp of his own left.

Ferguson threw his weight against Hazelthorne and both men went to the ground. Detrick held his breath. Rolling on the ground like that, with a naked knife thrashing back and forth, one of them was sure to get a serious wound if they weren't stopped soon.

But he didn't move. Like the other spectators he seemed frozen, unable to intervene.

He became aware of another voice, a shouting now plainly heard in the almost deathly silence that had replaced the racket of a few minutes before. Bowling men to right and left, Captain Garcia came charging into the ring. He didn't hesitate or pause. Running across the ring, he kicked savagely at Ferguson's arm, the one that held the knife.

The kick would certainly have made Ferguson drop the knife had it landed where it had been aimed. But so rapidly were the men rolling, that it missed and struck Hazelthorne's left arm instead. Hazelthorne released Ferguson's wrist with a howl. The knife plunged toward him.

Detrick held his breath. Garcia threw himself forward recklessly. For an instant Detrick thought he had been impaled on the knife. Then he realized that Garcia had succeeded in getting a grip on Ferguson's wrist. Savagely and angrily, Garcia twisted Ferguson's arm, forcing him to drop the knife.

Corporal Delaney moved in now, grabbing Ferguson's other arm. Between the two of them, Garcia and Delaney yanked Ferguson to his feet. The knife lay glittering on the ground. Hazelthorne got up, covered with dust and sweat and blood. He was panting raggedly. Garcia turned his head. "Go to your quarters, Sergeant." His voice had a quality that made Hazelthorne turn instantly and push his way through the thinning crowd.

Garcia didn't seem to have seen Colonel Detrick. To Delaney he said, "Put him in the guardhouse, Corporal."

"Yes, sir." With Ferguson's arm held high against the man's shoulderblades, Delaney marched him away.

Garcia said, "Fighting's over. Break it up!"

The men melted away into the darkness, talking softly among themselves. Garcia looked at Colonel Detrick. He said, "It's that damn woman, sir. Hazelthorne's wife."

"Yes." Detrick hesitated an instant. Then, saying, "Thank you, Captain," he turned and walked back across the parade, thankful for the darkness which might keep Garcia and the men from noticing that he couldn't walk very straight.

He reached the gallery and went into his quarters. He slammed the door behind him.

He had been first to reach the fighting men. He was the

one who should have halted it. When his shouted commands to stop had proved ineffective, he should have intervened physically.

But he hadn't and Garcia had. Garcia had come out of it looking like a hero and he had only seemed indecisive and ineffectual.

Was it going to be like that on this campaign! Cursing angrily beneath his breath, he crossed the room and poured himself another drink.

# CHAPTER 7

Ordered to his quarters, Tim Hazelthorne walked along the gallery and stepped inside. Blood ran from the cut on his forearm and dripped off the ends of his fingers. In the light of the lamp, he examined the cut and discovered, to his relief, that it was shallow and not serious. He got a clean flour-sack towel, ripped it into strips, and laid the strips on the table. He got the brown bottle and poured tequila over the wound. It burned like fire and he gritted his teeth until the worst of the pain had passed.

Lela came in. Without being asked, she crossed the room, picked up the strips of cloth and began to bandage her husband's arm.

He looked at her furiously but she would not glance up and meet his eyes. He said, "You bitch!"

She raised her glance and her eyes met his. For an instant there was an expression in her eyes that he had never seen before. Then the mocking look came back.

She said nothing until she had finished bandaging his arm. Then she walked away, letting her hips sway provocatively. The way her thin cotton dress was stuck to her with perspiration, he could see every muscle as she did.

Hazelthorne gritted his teeth. He picked up the bottle and took a drink. He said, "Damn you, you'd better walk the straight and narrow while I'm gone or I'll beat the hell out of you when I get back."

She turned her head. There was a lazy smile on her mouth and her lips were parted. "The straight and narrow is for dried-up old maids. Do I look like a dried-up old maid?"

Hazelthorne knew she was egging him on. He stared at her with frank puzzlement. "You're really askin' for it," he growled. But he was wondering why. Did she want to be beaten? He couldn't believe she did. But why else would she provoke him this way?

He asked, "What the hell's the matter with you anyway? Why do you have to be like this? What do you want from me?"

The mocking smile faded. For an instant there was both anger and bitterness in her face. She started to speak, then stopped. He said, "Go on. Say it."

"All right. I'll say it. You think a woman likes this God-forsaken place? It's hotter than hell most of the time and there's nothing to do but cook for you and do those fancy officers' dirty laundry. And the sun puts lines in a woman's face and makes her old before her time."

"Other people put up with it. What am I supposed to do?"

"You could get yourself transferred to some post back east. But oh no, not you. You like it here. Well, let me tell you something, Tim Hazelthorne. If I'm going to be stuck out here getting old, then I'm going to have all the fun I can. And if that means other men, then you're going to have to make the best of it."

For several moments Hazelthorne stared at her, scowling. His blood was still pumping at a faster-than-usual rate because of the fight with Ferguson. Now his manhood wouldn't permit him to hear such outright defiance from his wife without doing something about it.

He crossed the room toward her, his face ugly with frustration and anger. Shrilly and defiantly she screamed, "God damn you, go ahead! Hit me!"

He did. In the mouth with his fist. She went backwards and out through the open door onto the gallery. She sprawled on her back, mouth bleeding, eyes stricken and looking at him with disbelief.

They had been married seven years and this was the first time he had actually struck her. He was sorry and he wanted to go to her and tell her so but pride would not permit it. She had been wrong. She had tormented him beyond endurance. If he humbled himself now she would only have less respect for him.

She watched him without moving or trying to get up for what seemed like a long, long time. Then, realizing he did not intend to pursue her or hit her again, she got up and began to scream hysterical imprecations at him.

The noise brought the corporal of the guard and, a few minutes later, Garcia, hastily shrugging into his tunic. Garcia saw the blood trickling from one corner of Lela's mouth but he was more concerned with Hazelthorne's arm. To the corporal he said, "Take him down to the surgeon and make sure that arm is all right. Then put him in the guardhouse until morning."

Hazelthorne did not resist. Meekly he walked ahead of the corporal toward the post hospital.

Garcia gave Lela a long, level stare. Then he turned on his heel and walked back across the parade.

For a long time she stood there on the gallery, staring after him. The night air still was hot, but a light breeze stirring made her feel a little cooler than she had been inside the house. She raised a hand and felt her mouth, already getting puffy from her husband's blow.

Limply she went inside. In spite of the heat, she closed the door. She sat down and stared emptily at the floor.

Tim had asked, in desperation, what she wanted from him. Now she asked herself the same question. What *did* she want from him? Well, for one thing she wanted to get away from here.

She felt tears burning behind her eyes. She clenched her fists angrily. She wasn't going to cry! Damn it, she would not cry!

Then, suddenly, the tears came like a flood. She got up, ran to the bed, and threw herself down upon it full length. Wildly and bitterly she sobbed, seemingly unable to stop.

Tim was leaving at daybreak on a campaign that could not help but be perilous. He believed the Apaches had kidnapped Mrs. Detrick for the purpose of drawing the troops out of the fort.

Maybe he was right and maybe he was wrong. But right or wrong, he would leave tomorrow with the quarrel and her taunts that had caused it fresh in his mind. Memory of her threats would fester in his thoughts all the time that he was gone. He would never believe that she hadn't carried through on them when he got back. *If* he got back. Quite possibly he would not come back at all.

What would she do if he did not? she wondered. Well, she thought bitterly, she would be sent back east. Wasn't that what she had told him she wanted more than anything?

Still sobbing occasionally, she got up. She dried her eyes and licked her swollen lips. She wanted to see Tim and tell him she was sorry, but she knew it was impossible. Garcia, who apparently was officer of the day, would never permit it. Not at this time of night. She'd already caused too much trouble.

But Tim would have to come back here in the morning.

To pick up his things, things he'd need on the campaign.

She'd have a few minutes to talk with him. The trouble was that by morning his anger would have hardened, his outrage increased. She had made a fool of him in front of the entire complement of the fort. That wouldn't be easy for him to forgive.

Bleakly she stared at the whitewashed adobe wall. She didn't have much hope but she would try. She didn't think she could face a life that did not include Tim Hazelthorne.

Private Bruce Jenkins, of C Troop, slept not at all that night. He lay wide awake on his cot, staring at the ceiling above his head. Just turned eighteen, he had never seen action. He had never been in any kind of fight, not even with his fists.

Private Jenkins was scared. But as strong as his fear was his determination that it should never show. Whatever happened, he would perform the way he was expected to perform. He drew his pay, little as it was, for soldiering. Tomorrow he would begin to earn that pay. Soldiering.

Stories were plentiful around the fort about what savage fighters the Apaches were. Equally plentiful were the stories of what Apaches did to hapless whites who happened to fall into their hands.

Jenkins, along with everybody else at the fort, had seen the bodies of the escort troopers piled in the back of the ambulance; they were the first dead men he had ever seen. He would not forget the way their faces had looked as long as he lived.

He sweated and then he chilled. About two in the morning, the man on the cot next to him suddenly sat up and rolled himself a cigarette. The match illuminated Private

Buck Hutchcroft's face as he lighted it. It was sombre but otherwise expressionless.

Jenkins swung his legs over the edge of his cot and sat up too. Hutchcroft passed him the Bull Durham sack. Jenkins rolled himself a smoke with only indifferent success, spilling more than he used because of the way his hands were trembling. Hutchcroft said, "Scared?"

Shakily Jenkins grinned. "Does it show that much?"

"Be somethin' wrong with you if you wasn't scared."

"Are you?"

"Huh-uh. I been waitin' damn near a year for this crack at 'em."

Hutchcroft was, Jenkins guessed, about twenty-five. He didn't talk much and his face was usually as expressionless and dour as it was right now. Moonlight reflecting up from the floor highlighted it and gave it increased inscrutability. Jenkins waited, hoping Hutchcroft would go on. Listening to someone talk would, he knew, dull the fear in him.

Finally, speaking softly so as not to disturb the other sleepers in the room, Hutchcroft said, "I had me a girl before I joined up. She lived on a ranch back in the mountains about fifty miles north of Tucson. I was working for a freight company an' I only got out to see her about once every couple of months. I kep' tryin' to get her to marry me and come live in Tucson, but her pa kep' sayin' she was a mite too young. I was worried about them damn Apaches but he said he got along with 'em all right. Well, he was wrong. They killed him and his wife and my girl and her two brothers and left their house a pile of ashes. They . . ." He stopped. Jenkins could see that Hutchcroft's hands were trembling.

"They staked the two women out. . . ." He stopped again, and then he muttered so low that Jenkins could scarcely hear, "Oh, God damn their souls to hell!" Despite its softness, there was a bitter intensity to his voice.

In the silence that followed, Jenkins could hear only the breathing of the other men sleeping in the room. Finally Hutchcroft said, "Well, I made up my mind right there that I was goin' to spend the rest of my life killin' Apache Indians. I signed up with the army because I figured it was where I'd get the best chance of doin' it. So far I ain't killed me a single Indian. But tomorrow that's goin' to change." There was fierce elation in his voice.

Jenkins discovered that listening to Hutchcroft had lessened his own fear. Hutchcroft got up and began to pace back and forth in his bare feet like a caged animal.

Jenkins stared at him, puzzled and confused. He hadn't been here at the time of the attack on the Indian village at Arroyo Blanco but he had heard about it. He knew the village had been peaceful, the attack unprovoked. Just like the attack on the little ranch that Hutchcroft had told about.

But he didn't need to worry *his* head about who was right and who was wrong. He'd be busy enough keeping himself alive. And that meant shooting Indians. He wished daylight would come. He wished they were already on their way. He sensed that movement and action would lessen his fear better than anything else ever could.

# CHAPTER 8

It was still completely dark when reveille sounded across the parade. Immediately there were sounds of activity as the men belonging to B, C, and K Troops rolled out, dressed, and began to ready themselves for the campaign.

Mess call sounded thirty minutes later. By this time, most of the men were in the stable area, catching and saddling their mounts. Leaving what they were doing, they trooped to the mess hall. There was a lot of shouting back and forth, unabashed exhilaration at the promised activity after long months of inactivity and boredom.

Shaver ate in the mess hall as he usually did, as dour and uncommunicative as usual.

A guard brought breakfast to Hazelthorne, in the guardhouse, and then went to Hazelthorne's quarters to get the things he would need during the campaign. After a night of brooding, Tim Hazelthorne was bitterly angry at his wife. He had no intention of making up with her before he left.

Private Jenkins ate with trembling hands, keeping them out of sight as much as possible so that nobody would notice their trembling. Afterward, he headed back toward the stables to finish readying his horse.

Released from the guardhouse after finishing his breakfast, and having been warned not to go near his wife, Tim Hazelthorne also headed toward the stables.

The sky was beginning to gray faintly in the east when

the three troops began to form on the parade. There was a lot of confusion at first, but gradually order began to come out of the confusion as each man found his place.

These men were armed with Springfield single-shot carbines, .45 caliber, Model 1873. Why frontier troops, expected to fight Indians, were not equipped with available repeating carbines like the Spencer, nobody knew, except that it was typical of army inefficiency. As easy to explain would have been the frontier policy toward the Indians, which ranged from conciliation in the form of agents selected from clergymen of various religious groups to the offering of bounties for the hostiles' scalps.

Gradually the sky grew lighter. As the troops formed on the parade, those remaining behind gathered on the galleries to watch. Among these was Lela Hazelthorne, her eyes red from weeping, trying to pick out her husband from among all those crowding the open area. Ferguson was still in the guardhouse.

Garcia, mounted on his favorite bay, rode to Hazelthorne. "How's the arm this morning, Sergeant?"

"All right, Captain. Hardly hurts at all."

"What did the surgeon say about it? Did he think you'd be all right to go?"

"Yes, sir." There was a sudden cloud on Hazelthorne's face as he faced the possibility he might be left behind.

"Go say good-bye to your wife, Hazelthorne."

It was an order, one Hazelthorne knew he could not refuse to obey. He looked at Garcia pleadingly for an instant, but Garcia's expression remained adamant. Sullenly, Hazelthorne turned his horse and rode to where his wife was standing in front of their quarters. He said, "The captain told me to say good-bye to you."

Tears welled up in her eyes. There was neither mockery

nor defiance in her face today. She said, in a voice he could scarcely hear, "I'm sorry, Tim."

He sat his horse looking down at her for a moment, uncertainty plain in his face. He wanted to get off the horse and take her in his arms but he was acutely conscious that nearly every man on the parade was watching them. So he said instead, "I'll put in for a transfer when I get back."

The tears spilled across her pale cheeks. She managed a wan smile. Tim Hazelthorne said, "Good-bye."

"Good-bye, Tim." She watched him whirl his horse and ride back to his troop.

Detrick came from his quarters and mounted his horse, which his orderly was holding ready for him at the edge of the parade. He rode out to the center of the parade and faced the three troops, drawn up in lines that were less than straight because of the fidgeting of nervous horses. He glanced toward the stable area, where two supply wagons, an ammunition wagon, and an ambulance, each drawn by four mules, waited. Beyond them was a cluster of pack mules, thirty in all, in case the going got too rough for wagons, which at some time or other it most certainly would.

Shaver joined Detrick as he bawled the order to move out by twos. Captain Garcia and Sergeant Hazelthorne rode behind Shaver and Detrick, with C Troop strung out behind. B Troop followed C, and K Troop brought up the rear. Behind K Troop came the three wagons and the ambulance, and behind them came the mules, their packsaddles and heavily loaded panniers swaying from side to side whenever they broke into a trot.

Blinding clouds of dust rose from the cavalcade, which, fully extended, stretched out for nearly half a mile. Lela Hazelthorne peered through the lifting dust until Tim was lost to view. Then, with her shoulders slumping, she turned and went inside.

Why was she so bitchy? she asked herself. She had no satisfactory answer to that question. Much of the time, her actions and her words were compulsive, done without thought, in the hope of stinging Tim into some kind of response. Wisely or unwisely, when she wanted him to pay more attention to her she made him jealous. That was what she'd done last night, and look what the consequences had been.

The truth was, she didn't really know what she wanted or what made her so dissatisfied. Perhaps she saw youth slipping away and maybe she was trying to turn that process around. To get something out of life she didn't have and maybe sensed she would never have.

One thing she did know for sure. She hated this barren desert and she hated the heat and the isolation of it. She hadn't been to a town since coming here. She hadn't been able to buy a new dress and there wouldn't have been any place to wear it even if she had.

Tim had his friends. He had his work. She had these four walls, this stove, that wash tub and washboard, and the clothesline out back.

Maybe if they'd had children. . . . But they hadn't and wishing wasn't going to help. She hadn't the slightest idea whose fault it was. She doubted if it was Tim's. He was so strong, so masculine. She didn't see how it could be his fault.

And that meant the fault must be hers. Which didn't help her state of mind. But he had said he would put in for a transfer as soon as he got back.

*If* he got back, she thought. Lela did not often think of God, but she had come from a religious family. Now she began to pray silently that Tim would not be hurt or killed.

Not now, when there seemed to be a good chance that they'd be able to go back east and be happy again.

Colonel Detrick set a pace faster than the ambulance and wagons could maintain, knowing some time would necessarily be spent at the scene of yesterday's attack reading sign and establishing exactly what had happened there. The wagons would have time to catch up.

The wagons and ambulance fell farther and farther behind, but the mules kept pace. The sun was halfway up the sky when they reached the place. Detrick raised a hand, halting the column. Shaver rode ahead. Detrick followed and Garcia joined him.

Dismounted, Shaver moved slowly, eyes on the ground. He examined the spot where each of the escort troopers had been killed.

The dead horse with his cut harness marked the place where the ambulance had stopped. Shaver spent considerable time where the rear of the ambulance had been, but for the most part what tracks had been there had been wiped out by Roark, dragging and loading the bodies of the two troopers who had been bringing up the rear.

At the edge of the road, however, Shaver found what he had been looking for. He beckoned Garcia and Detrick, and pointed out the small print of one of Stephanie Detrick's shoes. He said, "She was dragged out of the ambulance. Right here she was boosted onto a horse, one of the horses the escort troopers had been riding."

"Then they must not have hurt her," Detrick said.

"Don't look like it."

"How many were there? Can you tell?"

"Not much closer than Roark said. Twenty or twenty-five maybe."

"Isn't that a lot for a raiding party?"

"Uh-huh."

Garcia hated to make suggestions, because he felt Detrick might refuse to accept them solely because they came from him, but he'd never know if he didn't find out now. He said, "Colonel, the wagons aren't here yet. Why don't we let Shaver backtrack these Indians to find out where they came from?"

"What difference does it make where they came from? What we're interested in is where they went."

"Might be interesting to know where they came from too, Colonel. Might be interesting to know if they were waiting here for Mrs. Detrick or if they just happened to run into the ambulance."

Detrick frowned, but he nodded his head. Garcia glanced at Shaver, surprised to see a look of reluctance on Shaver's face. But with a light shrug, Shaver mounted and began a large circle of the area. Garcia followed, realizing with some surprise that he was doing so because he did not trust Shaver to bring back the truth.

Shaver found the trail and followed it. Half a mile off the road he found the place where the Apaches had waited. He turned and glanced at Garcia. "You were right, Captain. They were waiting for the ambulance."

"How long did they wait? Can you tell?" Garcia had done a little trail reading of his own. He had spotted three separate campfires and there were many many tracks, scattered over an area more than a hundred yards in diameter. If he'd been asked how long they had waited he would have said several days.

Shaver was studying his face while he hesitated over his answer. Finally he said, "You've been reading the same tracks I have, Captain. They were here for several days."

"Then they had to have known Mrs. Detrick was coming. They had to have been waiting for her."

"I figure that way."

"Why? Do they want us to follow them?"

Shaver shrugged. "Maybe."

"Then they either intend to ambush us or they intend to attack the fort while most of the men are away from it chasing them."

Shaver shrugged again.

"Which do you figure it is?" Garcia persisted.

Shaver showed Garcia a totally expressionless face. "Neither one seems likely, to tell the truth. Apaches don't like head-on fights with cavalry. But of the two things I guess I'd have to say the fort."

Garcia nodded. "Go tell the colonel that." The decision was going to be Detrick's and Garcia knew what Detrick's decision was going to be. He couldn't give up the pursuit of the hostiles. They had killed four men and kidnapped his wife. He could hardly fail to pursue.

Shaver rode away toward the head of the column, where the colonel was waiting for him. Garcia followed more slowly, frowning with puzzlement. Shaver was right. Apaches didn't like head-on confrontations with cavalry. But they certainly seemed to be asking for one now.

But not immediately. Later, probably on ground of their own choosing at a time of their own choosing.

The wagons were approaching, about a quarter mile away. Detrick gave the command to move out. Shaver took the lead, following the hostiles' trail.

At noon they reached the site of the hostiles' first night's camp. Garcia all but held his breath as Shaver moved like a questing hound through the camp. Once he glanced at Detrick's face. The colonel's expression was tense but otherwise unreadable.

Finally Shaver returned. "Sign shows where one of 'em knocked her down, Colonel, but don't look like she was harmed any other way. They put her to gatherin' wood, like they would one of their own squaws."

A long breath of relief sighed out of Garcia. He realized how tense he had been, waiting for this word. Detrick also seemed to be relieved. He said, "Then they likely aren't going to hurt her if they have not already done so?"

"That'd be my guess, Colonel."

"And that means they took her to make us follow them."

Shaver nodded, watching the colonel's face. "Probably."

Garcia saw the satisfaction in the man. Shaver knew that Colonel Detrick believed three troops of cavalry could beat any concentration of Apaches that could be put together here. Shaver also knew that Detrick had no choice but to follow until he had made contact and either rescued his wife or verified her death.

# CHAPTER 9

One thing puzzled Garcia throughout the rest of the long, hot day. How had the Apaches known Mrs. Detrick was on the way? He supposed they could have learned of her impending arrival through talk overheard by English speaking "friendlies" in Lordsburg during the time the ambulance and escort had waited for her there.

In any case, he guessed it didn't matter how they had learned. What mattered was that they had and that they had successfully kidnapped her. They had ensured pursuit and presumably had some plan in mind. An ambush probably. But Garcia was sure the Indians would never attack three troops of cavalry unless they felt certain they could win.

They continued at a steady gait until sundown, when Colonel Detrick called a halt. Each troop commander supervised the care of his troop's horses. They were unsaddled, rubbed down, and given a ration of grain. They were watered sparingly and would be allowed to graze until dark, when they would be tethered to a picket line. Only after the horses had been taken care of did the men look to their own comfort.

The bugler blew taps half an hour after dark and guards were stationed around the bivouac. Garcia lay awake for a while, thinking of Stephanie in the hostiles' hands. He had noticed her hat in the ambulance after the bodies of the dead troopers had been lifted out, so he knew she was without a covering for her head. Her face and neck would sunburn cruelly. Her skin would blister.

By now she must be close to complete exhaustion. Yet tomorrow she would be forced to mount her horse and go on again. When there was work to be done she would have to do it or be beaten. The Apaches would use her up to the limit of her strength. Only if it appeared she might die would they let up on her.

He went to sleep finally. He awoke while it was still dark. The bugler was blowing reveille.

By the time it was light, the command was once more on the move. Riding out, Detrick asked Shaver, "How old are their tracks? Are they getting away from us?"

Shaver spurred his horse. He rode half a mile ahead so that he wouldn't halt the column and there dismounted to study the trail the hostiles had left. By the time the troops had caught up, he was sitting his horse waiting for them. Detrick looked questioningly at him.

Shaver said, "They're still far ahead, Colonel, according to their tracks. But I figure we'll find where they camped last night before very long."

"Does that mean we're gaining on them or losing ground?"

Shaver shrugged. "Keepin' up, Colonel. Ain't neither losing nor gaining ground."

Detrick nodded, satisfied. They were traveling now in a southwesterly direction. Despite the slight increase in altitude, the day gave promise of being nearly as hot as yesterday. The never-ending mountains marched away on all sides, lavender and rose-colored in the first light of sunrise.

Behind the column rose a towering pillar of dust. As heat built up and wind began to blow, dust devils, or whirlwinds, could be seen in the distance, sometimes raising dust to a height of a couple of hundred feet.

Sergeant Hazelthorne, riding beside Captain Garcia, wore a scowl on his broad and usually pleasant face. Garcia knew he was thinking about his wife. He wanted to try and reassure him but knew it would be useless and probably an unwanted intrusion into Hazelthorne's private affairs. In midmorning, however, Hazelthorne finally asked, "How long you reckon we'll be out, Captain?"

"Week or two. Why?"

"Well, I went an' said good-bye to my wife like you told me to. I reckon everybody on the whole post was watching on account of the fight the night before, so I couldn't really do it proper. But I guess maybe we had an understanding. My part was that I'd ask for a transfer back east just as soon as I got back. What I'd like to know is if you'll approve it, sir."

"I'll approve it, Sergeant. I'll do my best to get the colonel to approve it too. But I'll hate to see you go."

"Thank you, sir." There was relief in Hazelthorne's voice. He waited a moment before he said, "Them Indians are just leadin' us into some kind of trap, ain't they, sir?"

"Looks like it. Can't be much of a surprise, though, if we're on the lookout for it."

"No, sir."

After that they rode in silence, Garcia frowning now instead of Hazelthorne. They all knew there was some kind of ambush or trap waiting for them ahead. Since they knew, how could a surprise attack on them succeed?

About halfway back in C Troop Privates Jenkins and Hutchcroft rode side by side. Under the monotony and boredom of riding fourteen hours a day, Jenkins had been able to subdue the fear he had felt back at Fort Lincoln the

night before riding out. But it still lay there in the back of
his mind, along with a nagging doubt as to how he would
perform when the time finally came. He supposed no man
ever knew but, glancing aside at Hutchcroft, he realized
there were exceptions to that rule. Hutchcroft had no
doubts about himself. He was as eager as a hound on a trail
and he couldn't wait until they closed with their quarry and
he could begin to revenge the death of his promised bride
and her family.

Neither man had seen the hostiles' trail so they couldn't
know how broad and plain it was. Nor did they speculate on
the possibility that an ambush waited for the three troops
somewhere ahead. They left such things to the scout,
Shaver, and to the colonel.

Shortly before noon they came upon the last night's camp
of the hostiles, as Shaver had predicted they would. Swiftly,
Shaver scouted the area, afterward coming back to Colonel
Detrick with the word that again Stephanie had been sent
to gather firewood. Her steps, he said, had been faltering,
and once she had fallen, scattering her load of wood.

Garcia listened, studying the colonel's face. Impassive, it
showed him nothing of what the colonel was feeling. He
wondered if his own expression was equally impassive and
hoped it was.

Because he was sorrowing for Stephanie. She was ill
equipped for the ordeal she was now being forced to un-
dergo. She wasn't used to hard labor. She wasn't used to riding and she must be horribly saddlesore. She was pitilessly
exposed to the brilliant desert sun and every exposed por-
tion of her skin must be blistered and raw. Maybe by now
she had fashioned some kind of shelter for herself out of her
petticoat or skirt, but it would be days before her burned
skin stopped torturing her.

Besides her physical torture she must be growing increasingly troubled over the chances that she would be found and rescued. She had no way of knowing Private Roark's life had been spared, or that he had managed to get the ambulance to the fort. She had no way of knowing these three troops were following, intent on rescuing her. She must be feeling only bleak hopelessness as she faced a life that held nothing but hard physical labor, abuse, and perhaps even death.

Having inspected the Apaches' camp site, the column moved on, following a trail that now was only half a day old. It continued in a southwesterly direction and, while the Indians remained in the mountains, Garcia knew they could not now be far from the settlement of Tucson.

The day dragged on, with the command's progress slowed now by the supply wagons and the ambulance, which were ill able to traverse the rocky, mountainous terrain. At sundown the colonel finally halted to wait for the vehicles to catch up.

Shaver did not unsaddle his horse when the rest of the men did and Garcia, watching him, kept the saddle on his own mount, waiting to see what Shaver was going to do.

The scout led his horse down into the draw where troopers with shovels had managed to locate water. He let his horse drink, and drank himself, then rode out following the hostiles' trail.

Garcia waited until he had passed out of sight around a bend in the draw. Then he followed, hoping Colonel Detrick would not see and challenge him. He reached the bend in the draw and immediately breathed easier.

Ahead, he glimpsed Shaver just going out of sight around another bend. He held his horse to a slow walk, not wanting Shaver to discover him.

For a scout to go out in the evening and scout the trail they were following was not, in itself, suspicious. Garcia wondered what he expected of Shaver and why he was following. Did he suspect that Shaver had an alliance with the Indians? He shook his head. That was ridiculous. Shaver might have an Indian wife and two half-breed children but he took pay from the army and had for years. He would hardly betray his trust. But if it was not betrayal that Garcia suspected, what was it?

He halted his horse, hesitating, feeling foolish. What if Shaver caught him following? How could he explain himself?

On the point of turning back, he suddenly saw Shaver come into sight heading toward him.

He did, indeed, feel foolish. And he didn't know how he could explain himself. But he had been seen and there was no use wishing he had gotten away unseen.

Shaver approached at a steady walk. A dozen yards away he pulled his horse to a halt. "Looking for me, Captain?"

Garcia tried not to look as foolish as he felt. "Just came out to see if you found anything."

"Are you sure that was it, Captain?"

"What else would it be?"

"Could it be you think I'm in cahoots with the Apaches?"

"Are you?" Garcia didn't see any sense in beating around the bush. He did suspect Shaver, though exactly of what he didn't know.

"You don't think I'd tell you if I was, do you?"

"No." For several moments the two stared at each other. Shaver's face was without expression, yet there was a quality in the scout's eyes that was disturbing to Garcia. Shaver was, he decided, a complicated man, not nearly as simple as he seemed.

"You don't think these twenty-five Indians we're following could ambush three troops of cavalry?"

"I doubt it will be twenty-five for very long."

"Well, I don't think it will be either, Captain." Shaver was silent for a moment, staring steadily at Garcia all the while. At last he said, "Wouldn't follow anymore if I was you. Man in my business gets jumpy sometimes. Keeps him alive. Makes him too quick on the trigger, though. Surprise him and you might get shot."

Garcia met his look with an equally steady one. He said, "I won't get shot, Mr. Shaver."

Shaver touched his horse's sides with his heels. He rode past Garcia and headed back toward the bivouac. After a moment's frowning hesitation, Garcia followed him.

# CHAPTER 10

By the time the Apaches reached their second night's camp, Stephanie Detrick was close to complete exhaustion. Never before in her entire life had she been so tired, so miserable. The insides of her thighs were raw from the chafing of the cruel McClellan saddle. So was her seat. It had reached the point that she could not even shift position to ease the pain. She hurt every place where contact was made with the saddle.

In addition, her skin was blistered from the pitiless direct rays of the desert sun. Her lips were cracked and bleeding. Tonight she wished the Apaches would kill her and get it over with. When she dismounted she could not stand but collapsed in a heap. She lay there a moment, not caring what the Indians did to her.

None of them paid any attention to her. Numbly she thought that she must be so far gone they realized they'd get no work out of her tonight.

But they didn't want her to die, she knew. She had been taken for a reason and she would be no good to them if she was dead. Gradually rest and the lack of motion made her feel somewhat better and she raised her head.

They apparently wanted to be pursued and expected to be pursued. That meant her husband and his troopers were, probably, already on the trail. In time they would overtake and engage the Indians.

Instinctively she knew that, once her usefulness was at an end, the Apaches would kill her without a second thought. Therefore, if she wanted to survive, and she did despite the way she felt tonight, she had better keep herself in condition to escape successfully when the time for it came.

She struggled to her feet. She staggered to her horse and got the saddle off, then released him to join the others. She staggered away up the little draw to gather firewood.

She gathered two loads. After she had dumped the second on the ground, one of the Indians offered her a water bag. There was an expression on his face that looked to her like grudging respect. It made her feel stronger just seeing it. These Indians might be ignorant savages and they had kidnapped her, hurt her, killed the troopers escorting her. But somehow it made her feel good to know she had passed the test.

The same Apache who had given her a drink, pockmarked and squat, gave her some jerky too. She stumbled to her saddle, collapsed, and put her back to it.

When she had finished the jerky, she tore a piece of cloth from her petticoat and tied it over her head so that there was a flap in front to serve as a shade to protect her face from the sun in the days to come.

An Indian, apparently sent back to scout the progress of the pursuing cavalry, rode into camp at dark and, in guttural Apache reported to the others. There was some laughing and some remarks were made that were unmistakably derisive. Then the Apaches settled down to sleep.

Stephanie chilled in the night air. She didn't know if she had a fever or whether it was because of the contrast between day's pitiless heat and night's chill. Teeth chattering, she lay on the ground, trying to endure.

Half an hour passed. Finally one of the Indians got up

and tossed her a stinking blanket that had been used on the back of a horse. She pulled it over her gratefully, not even caring that its smell was overpowering. She went to sleep.

It seemed no more than a few minutes before one of the Apaches was stirring her with his foot. Another snatched the blanket. A third threw the McClellan saddle on her horse and cinched it down.

Wearily she climbed to the horse's back, wincing even before her chafed parts hit it. When they did, she almost screamed with the pain. But she knew that screaming, hysteria, or complaint would fall upon deaf ears. The only thing they would accomplish would be to lose her the grudging respect the Indians now were giving her.

The Indians moved out, and her horse followed along. Stephanie clenched her fists and jaws and endured the pain. At least, this morning, her face was partially shielded by the cloth she had bound around her head.

As she rode, she tore more strips from her petticoat and wrapped them around the backs of her blistered hands. Gradually, as movement loosened her up, she began to hurt less.

The trail steepened as they climbed into a range of rocky, barren mountains. Many times she was forced to hold on to the saddle as the horse lunged up some steep slope. And finally, in midafternoon, they reached an Apache village.

There were, she guessed, more than a hundred and fifty brush wickiups, so the village had to have been here for some time. Children ran back and forth, some entirely naked, some nearly so. Women moved purposefully about. Almost immediately Stephanie realized that they were abandoning this village. Horses were being hastily packed. Others were being caught out of the herd which had apparently just been driven in.

Indians, both men and women, surrounded Stephanie and the Apaches who had captured her. There was much talk, most of it excited, none of it understandable. The village Apaches stared curiously at her, but none offered her any harm.

The Indians who had captured her filled their water containers and replenished their supply of jerky. Some dismounted and disappeared for a short time. Some squatted in the shade of a few stunted trees that grew along the edge of the dry wash. Others just stretched and waited until their companions would be ready to go again. None of them indicated that she was to dismount, so she stayed in her saddle. She felt safer on the horse and she knew they would be leaving again soon anyway.

They had been in the village less than half an hour when all the men returned, mounted, and headed out again. Other groups were leaving the village, scattering, each heading in a different direction. She was thinking about tearing off a piece of her petticoat when one of the Indians rode up beside her, reached out, and tore a piece off himself. He dismounted and impaled it on a branch of ocotillo that stretched out across the trail.

Looking back, she saw it fluttering, plainly visible from the village site. It would lead the cavalry this way. Perhaps its purpose was to keep the soldiers from following any of the other groups. Or perhaps it would only lead them to the planned ambush. She wondered if she would still be alive when the time for the ambush came.

It was midmorning when the three troops of cavalry reached the site of the abandoned Apache village. Detrick, Shaver, and Garcia spotted the fluttering scrap of petticoat immediately. Detrick halted the column. Garcia sat with

Detrick while Shaver scouted the empty village on foot. He poked around, looked into several of the empty wickiups, stirred the fire ashes with a foot, then made a big circle of the village to pick up the various trails leaving it.

While he was working, each troop commander gave the order to dismount and loosen cinches. A few of the most conscientious of the men unsaddled and either fanned or rubbed their horses' backs. Those of the men who smoked lighted up and tried to find some shade.

Shaver was back in fifteen minutes. To Detrick he said, "They all pulled out of here in late afternoon yesterday, Colonel. Scattered like quail. Kind of knocks a hole in your theory that they're fixin' to ambush us."

"Which group has Mrs. Detrick? The one that left that scrap of cloth, or do you think that was left for a decoy?"

"Won't know until we find their first camp. Oughtn't to be too far ahead."

"Can't you tell from the tracks?"

"I can tell that the horse she had been ridin' went that way. I can't tell whether she was still ridin' it or not."

"All right. Let's go." Detrick waved his arm forward and commands rang out down the long line of weary troopers, who mounted and rode out.

The supply wagons and the ambulance had dropped even farther behind when the going became too rough for them.

Garcia watched Shaver suspiciously, wondering what was going on in his mind. Shaver had an Apache wife and two half-breed kids. That in itself implied a certain affinity with the Indians and did not rule out the idea that he had conspired with them to lead the soldiers into a trap.

To some extent, Garcia shared Detrick's belief that three troops of U. S. Cavalry could whip just about any Indian force that could be thrown against them. That idea, however, depended on the assumption that, at the time of battle, the U.S. troops were in good condition, well armed and supplied. But suppose, at the time of battle, the troopers were at the point of exhaustion? Suppose they were low on food and morale. Suppose their horses were worn out?

Already the wagons and the ambulance had been allowed to drop behind. They would, presumably, catch up tonight. But eventually, if the trail continued through these steep and rugged mountains, the supply wagons were going to have to be abandoned altogether.

The command moved along, with Shaver riding ahead now by a hundred yards or so, studying the trail carefully as he rode. Less than an hour had passed when he halted suddenly. Dismounting, he studied the ground, walking forward slowly. After scouting around for several minutes, he mounted his horse and rode back to Colonel Detrick, who had halted the column. Shaver said, in a voice that carried to Garcia's ears, "She's with 'em all right, Colonel. I found her footprints where they stopped to rest."

"Thank you, Mr. Shaver." He hesitated a moment and then he asked, "What do you think, Mr. Shaver? Are we going to have to contend with only this small group or do you think we will be ambushed as Mr. Garcia suspects?"

Shaver said, "Don't look like no ambush now, Colonel. Looks to me like this bunch happened onto that ambulance and jumped it just for the hell of it. When they found out your wife was in the ambulance, they took her. But I think all we got to worry about is twenty or twenty-five Indians."

Garcia rode forward. "If that's so, why have they refrained from treating her the way Indians usually treat the white women they capture?"

Shaver shrugged.

Garcia said, "Looks funny to me. Here's twenty or

twenty-five male Indians, with a female captive. If they'd wanted her for a slave wouldn't they have left her with the people in that village?"

Shaver's glance was wary. "I can't read them Indians' minds, Captain."

Detrick was watching Garcia, occasionally switching his glance to Shaver.

Garcia said, "I've got a feeling we don't need a scout, Colonel. I've got a feeling anyone could follow this trail because they don't want us to lose it. It's like riding down a road and you and I both know that when the Apaches want to hide a trail they hide it so well that it takes an expert to follow it."

Detrick looked at Shaver. "What about that, Mr. Shaver?"

Shaver said, "They don't know they're being followed, Colonel, so why should they hide their trail? They likely figured they killed Private Roark as well as the four guards."

Garcia asked, "Then why did the people in that village scatter like a bunch of quail?"

Shaver looked at Colonel Detrick. "Colonel, do you want me to stay? If you don't, I'll leave right now."

Garcia, because of a warning look from Detrick, kept still. He believed, even if the colonel did not, that if Shaver did leave it would not be to go back. Shaver would, if he left the troops, ride ahead and join the Indians. For some reason, unknown to Garcia, Shaver was a traitor, trying to deliver the three troops of cavalry into the Indians' hands. But he had no proof and, even if he had, he felt it would be better to keep Shaver where he could be watched than to let him join the Indians.

Detrick said, "Of course we want you to stay, Mr. Shaver." He turned his glance on Garcia. "In the future you are not to question Mr. Shaver's loyalty. Is that clear, Mr. Garcia?"

Garcia nodded. "Yes, sir." But privately he retained his doubts. He might not be able to question Shaver verbally. But he intended to watch every move that Shaver made. Maybe by doing so he would know when the Apache attack would come.

Of one thing he was sure. The Apaches would not attack until the troopers were near exhaustion, until they were easy prey.

# CHAPTER 11

From this point, the Apaches' trail climbed along an ever-roughening route into the barren, furnace-hot mountains. Horses toiled upward, lunging on the steepest slopes, lathered and wheezing by the time they reached a small, level clearing at noon.

Colonel Detrick, realizing that the wagons and ambulance would never be able to negotiate this murderous terrain, sent half a dozen troopers back with instructions for the wagons to return to the last water and wait there for the rest of the command to return. The troopers were to remain with the wagons as a guard.

In Captain Garcia, uneasiness began to increase. Studying Colonel Detrick's face, however, he could detect no sign of matching uneasiness in it. He walked through the resting, lounging men, assessing both their condition and that of their mounts.

So far, the men themselves, while plainly tired and hot, showed little sign of exhaustion. But their mounts were something else. There wasn't a horse in the entire command that wasn't lathered from the long, hot, torturous climb. Some of them were still trembling even after they had been halted fifteen minutes. Most stood with their heads down, lacking the spirit even to crop at the scant vegetation that grew in the shelter of rocks and the various cactus plants.

Garcia returned to his own horse. Hazelthorne had pulled

the saddle off and was fanning the back of the captain's horse. His own mount stood nearby, awaiting similar treatment. Garcia noted that Hazelthorne had seen to it that all of C Troop's horses had received the same care.

Hazelthorne, his face beet red, said, "Couple of dry camps, Captain, and these horses ain't goin' to be good for anything."

Garcia had been thinking the same thing, but he said reassuringly, "The Indians need water too."

"Not as much as us. When they wear out a horse they raid a ranch and steal a fresh one. Then they kill the one they been ridin' and pack along part of his hindquarters to eat."

Garcia didn't reply. He turned away, trying not to let his own concern over the situation show. The Indians couldn't have picked a better ploy for ensuring stubborn pursuit by the cavalry. With his wife in the hands of the savages, Colonel Detrick simply couldn't quit. He would go on far past the point he would ordinarily consider prudent. He would, in fact, go on until his troops were no longer an effective fighting force. That was what the Apaches would be waiting for and, when that time came, they would attack.

Garcia tried to talk himself out of this gloomy certainty, but however he tried he failed. Fatalistically, he accepted what was happening because he knew nothing he could say or do would change anything. Detrick would not turn back. And Garcia wasn't at all convinced that, had he been in command, he would have turned back himself. Stephanie's life depended upon their rescuing her. If the cavalry turned back, the Indians would kill her immediately, because she would be of no further use to them.

After an hour's rest, Detrick gave the command to move out and the column formed again and raggedly followed him. Mercifully, the trail descended sharply for a while. Several of the horses, still trembling from the climb, stumbled and fell at particularly treacherous spots. Fortunately none of the horses or their riders sustained any injury.

Steadily the trail descended until, in midafternoon, they reached a narrow valley, watered by a narrow, brackish stream. Horses lined up at it, sucking up the water noisily until forced to desist by their riders, who knew that too much water would disable them.

They took half an hour in this spot, watering horses, filling canteens, and letting the horses graze. Then Detrick ordered them on and repetitions of his order echoed and re-echoed down the line.

The trail now followed this narrow, grassy valley southward and half an hour later they glimpsed a small ranch ahead.

The buildings appeared deserted. There was no sign of life except for a few Rhode Island Red chickens scratching in the yard. With dismal certainty, Garcia knew what they were going to find waiting for them when they reached the small adobe shack.

The gate of the adobe corral stood open. The rancher, bearded and about fifty years old, lay face up in the sun immediately in front of the shack. His shirt front was a mass of dried blood, around which buzzed a swarm of blue-bodied flies. There was a boy, maybe fifteen years old, a dozen yards away, also dead.

Shaver got down and went into the cabin. He emerged a few moments later. "No women, Colonel. From the looks of the place, it was a man's layout." He crossed to the corral and read the tracks at the gate. Looking up he said, "They got about a dozen horses. Looks like maybe these two had been breakin' broncs."

Detrick glanced at Garcia. "Detail a burial party, Captain."

Garcia nodded at Hazelthorne, who barked out half a dozen names. The men got a couple of shovels from a shed and a couple more from the pack mules bringing up the rear. They went to work, changing off often because of the blistering heat.

Detrick ordered that the bodies and the cabin be searched for anything that might establish the identity of the dead man and boy so that the Army could attempt to notify survivors.

Garcia directed that the man and boy be wrapped in a couple of army burial sheets, which were laced up afterward. When the graves were ready half an hour later, Detrick stood at the graveside and spoke a few words over the bodies before they were lowered in.

The command moved out again. It was now late afternoon. At a lagging walk, the long column moved down the valley. The sun sank low in the western sky.

Five miles after leaving the cabin, they sighted a second cabin about a mile ahead. Knowing what they were going to find, Detrick did not even pick up the pace. The Apaches had been through here this morning. They had left no one alive at the last cabin and it was not reasonable to expect anyone to be alive at the next.

Traveling in this nearly level valley was, however, good for the horses. The sweat had dried on their necks and flanks. Their heads were raised and now and then one cropped at a clump of grass.

Garcia kicked his horse in the ribs and rode forward to join Colonel Detrick and Shaver. He said, "Colonel, we're going to find some more bodies up ahead. Couldn't we leave a burial detail behind and make a forced march? Might be we'd catch the Indians where they make camp tonight."

Detrick scowled, but the scowl faded. He looked at Shaver. "What do you think?"

Shaver said, "Your horses are in bad shape, Colonel. The Indians got maybe a dozen fresh ones at that last place and they probably got some more at that cabin up ahead. Don't look to me like wearin' your horses out now would be very smart."

Detrick glanced at Garcia. "I think Shaver's right."

Garcia didn't argue because he knew it would do no good. Besides, he had to admit there was logic in Shaver's argument. At the same time, he thought there was equal logic in his own suggestion. Catching this small group of Indians now might save a confrontation later with a larger group, when the command would be exhausted and their mounts in worse shape than they were right now.

He returned to his place at the head of his troop. Both Corporal Delaney and Sergeant Hazelthorne were watching him. So was Scott Martell, the lieutenant, riding about half-way back. Martell was a young man, inexperienced but steady and dependable.

They reached the small cabin. Here, too, the corral gate was open. A man of about forty lay dead before the cabin. An elderly woman, perhaps the dead man's mother, lay sprawled thirty or forty yards away. Blood had soaked the back of her head from a blow, apparently inflicted as she tried futilely to reach the safety of the shack.

Garcia studied Shaver's face, his eyes questioning. He asked, "Just the two of them, or did the man have a wife?"

Shaver went into the cabin and Garcia followed. Shaver poked around, picking up pieces of clothing, studying them, putting them down again. He opened a trunk and rummaged through the contents of it. Turning finally, he said, "There was another woman here, likely his wife. Looks like the Indians took her along with them."

Garcia experienced a feeling of revulsion and disgust. Obviously the Apaches had taken the woman from here because they wanted her but didn't want to take any time with her here. They'd carry her along with them to wherever they camped tonight. Tomorrow that was where her body would be found.

Burning, bitter hatred, greater than any he had ever felt before, began to grow in Garcia's mind. Right now it wasn't hard for him to understand the savage, sometimes almost irrational hatred felt by whites in this area toward the Apache Indians. He could understand their belief that the only solution to the Indian problem was extermination of the Indians.

Yet uneasily in the back of his mind was the memory of what he had heard about Colonel Detrick's attack two years ago on the peaceful Apache village at Arroyo Blanco. In a more rational frame of mind he would have been forced to admit that there were two sides to everything. The way he felt now he wasn't inclined to be either charitable or reasonable. All he wanted was for this column of troops to close with the Indians they were pursuing. He wanted the Indians wiped out like a nest of rats.

Detrick now bawled an order for Captain Schofield of B Troop to come forward. He directed Schofield to detail a burial party to remain here and bury the bodies of the man and the old woman. Once more, he had all available papers collected so that survivors, if any, of the dead could be notified. He waved the column forward and rode out again, still heading south.

Less than half a mile below the cabin, the Apaches' trail left the valley and climbed a steep and barren slope into the mountains again. Garcia supposed that they were familiar with this area and knew there were no more ranches ahead. Again the cavalry mounts lunged up the slope in the blistering late-afternoon heat, and were sweated and lathered by the time they reached the top.

Detrick halted them, allowing ten minutes for them to rest. His face, which Garcia studied carefully, showed the frustration that he felt. He knew he was wearing his men's horses out. He was facing the possibility that sooner or later they were going to have to turn back, before the horses were so exhausted they couldn't make it back to the fort.

Despite his distrust of Detrick, Garcia felt a certain sympathy for him. The colonel couldn't quit, and if he went on he faced the possibility of disaster and the loss of his command. He was being torn between the obligation to rescue his wife and his responsibility to his men.

But, combined with that obvious frustration in Detrick's face, was something else that troubled Garcia. It was a quality that could only be described as frantic and Garcia couldn't help wondering what increasing pressure in the days to come would do to Detrick's ability to function as commander of these three troops.

After the ten minutes were up, the command moved out again.

The terrain here was murderous, a series of hills and ravines that meant the column was either descending into a ravine or climbing out of one. To make matters worse, the ravines collected the sun's heat and there was scarcely any breeze on the tops of the ridges to cool either the horses or the men.

Detrick halted the column for ten minutes out of every hour but, despite this care, the horses grew increasingly weaker until several were losing their footing and falling on every downslope.

As plainly as if it had been written out for him, Garcia could see the Apaches' strategy. There were easier ways to travel if all they had wanted to do was get from one place to another. Even if they were aware of the pursuit, there were better ways of getting away, if that was what they wanted. Obviously it was not.

At sundown they came upon a dead horse. The better part of one hindquarter was gone, and flies were laying eggs in the exposed areas of flesh. Half a dozen vultures rose from the carcass as the command approached.

Darkness found them still in the same rough, dry country. They made a dry camp where there was scarcely enough level ground for the men to stretch out and sleep. And since there was nothing but cactus in the area, it was a cold camp as well, with the men munching on hardtack and washing it down sparingly with what water they had left.

Lying staring at the stars, Garcia wondered gloomily if Stephanie was still alive. He admitted the possibility that when they found the ravaged body of the ranch woman tomorrow they would find Stephanie's body too.

# CHAPTER 12

The following day dawned bright and clear. Not a cloud was visible in the sky and even before the sun came up it was insufferably hot. It had not, in fact, fallen below ninety degrees throughout the night.

Outwardly the routine was the same, except of course that there was no water but that which remained in the men's canteens and in the water casks carried by half a dozen of the mules and as yet untapped.

But Garcia detected a difference, a subtle one, in the attitudes of the men. He heard some grumbling. He witnessed some sharp exchanges between troopers that stopped just short of coming to blows.

As the command moved out, Hazelthorne joined Garcia at the head of C Troop and glanced at him ruefully. Softly, so that he would not be overheard, he said, "They're gettin' pretty edgy, sir."

"I noticed."

"They're sayin' why should they all be killed to rescue a couple of women, even if one of them is the colonel's wife."

"What makes them think they're going to be killed? We've only got twenty or so Indians ahead of us."

"They figure it ain't going to stay that way. They figure all the bucks in that village we came through are going to be waiting for us up ahead someplace."

There was some stiffness in Garcia's voice as he said,

"They're soldiers, damn it! They'll do what they're told!"

"Yes, sir." An equal stiffness was in Hazelthorne's voice.

Garcia gave him a spare smile. "Nobody told them soldiering out here was going to be easy. Nobody told them they'd always win."

"No, sir." The reply was noncommittal, but Garcia knew the strain that had been between them a moment before was gone.

He couldn't reveal his own doubts to Hazelthorne. Like the greenest buck private in the command, he had to obey Detrick's orders even if he didn't agree with them.

Unless he could come up with more than the vague suspicions he had now. Even if he did, he couldn't be sure Detrick would turn back. He couldn't even be sure he would want the colonel to, no matter how bad things got. Turning back would ensure Stephanie's death, a prolonged and painful one.

The truth was, they were between a rock and a hard place and very probably nothing they did would come out right. Worst of all was the underlying fear in Garcia's mind that it was for nothing. Barring a miracle, Stephanie would be dead when the battle was over, anyway.

Again today the Indians deliberately led the pursuing cavalry up and down, up and down, in country as blistering hot and dry as it was rough. The colonel continued to halt for ten minutes out of every hour to give the horses rest.

It was not until the noon halt that real trouble broke out. Garcia heard shouting back in the direction of K Troop. He paid it little heed, even though the voice tones were obviously angry ones. It was not his business. Captain Healy, commanding K, would handle it.

Only when he heard a shot did he break into a run toward the sound. Ahead of him other men were also running. It took Garcia, closely followed by Colonel Detrick, several minutes to force his way through the gathering crowd.

When he did reach the small cleared circle, he was shocked by what he saw. A trooper lay on his back on the ground, a bloodstain spreading on the front of his sweaty shirt. The man was dead. Being held by two K Troop noncoms was another man, his face dripping sweat, his eyes wild. Captain Healy glanced at Colonel Detrick. He said, "Fight, Colonel."

"Put that man in irons. Assign a burial detail to take care of the dead one. I want a full report of what happened, along with the statements of witnesses."

"Yes, sir."

Detrick turned and pushed his way back through the crowd. Garcia followed him. What had happened was probably only the first of other such incidents. Heat, exhaustion, and thirst would continue to take their toll of the men's morale. Knowledge that the killer would be tried and executed upon return to the fort might deter some but it would not deter them all.

When he reached the head of his own troop, Garcia studied Hiram Shaver's face. It was impassive but he could not escape the feeling that Shaver was very pleased.

Detrick allowed an extra fifteen minutes for the dead man to be buried. Healy would, he knew, conduct a short burial service before they went on.

The afternoon dragged. Mercifully they finally came out of the extremely rough country through which they had been traveling and began to climb more gradually toward a high range of mountains directly south of them. Garcia knew Mexico could not be much farther ahead. He wondered what the colonel would do when they reached the border. Officially Detrick was not permitted to cross, but the border was not marked or defined here as it was farther east by the Rio Grande. Detrick could always claim he had not realized the border had been crossed.

The camp, tonight, was dry again. Detrick directed Shaver to scout ahead and see if water was available within a reasonable distance. Garcia watched him go, wanting to follow but doubting both the wisdom and effectiveness of doing so. Shaver would be watching his back trail and if he did follow, Shaver was sure to catch him at it.

He walked among the men, studying them without seeming to, saying a word or two of encouragement here and there. The men were tired and they were hot. They were edgy and irritable but they were far from the point where they would cease to be an effective fighting force. There would be more fights but the majority of the men would keep themselves under control.

The horses were another matter. Garcia, accompanied by Hazelthorne, walked the length of C Troop's picket line, studying the condition of their mounts.

They each had already been given a morral of oats. They had been watered sparingly from the kegs carried on the mules. But the amount of grain and water they had been given was grossly inadequate. These horses had hardly enough stamina in them to last two more days. Unless they got rest and enough water and food, they were going to start giving out.

C Troop had two farriers and he directed them to inspect the shoes of every horse. Better to find loose shoes before they were thrown than afterward.

Just at dusk, Captain Healy of K Troop and Schofield of B, came to him where he was readying himself to sleep. Both men's faces looked sheepish in the flickering firelight. Perhaps because it was late, they wasted no time with preliminaries. Schofield, a tall, gaunt man, said, "We've been talking. We've both been looking over the horses in our troops and if they go more than another day, they're not going to make it back."

Garcia said, "There's no alternative. Not if we expect to get the colonel's wife back alive."

The two men were silent a moment and then Healy said, "Is one woman worth this whole command?"

Garcia reminded gently, "Four men were killed when they took her."

Healy said, "I don't know about your men, but mine are doing a lot of grumbling. They're saying we ought to turn back. If we don't, I can tell you one thing. There'll be more fights like the one in K Troop today."

"What have you got in mind?"

"I think the three of us ought to go to the colonel. We ought to tell him what we think."

Garcia shook his head. "It wouldn't do any good. They've got his wife. They killed four troopers getting her. He can't give up. Anyway, it's not a question of weighing things. We're out here to keep the Apaches under control. Not only did they kill four troopers and kidnap the colonel's wife. They killed the people back there at those two ranches we passed yesterday. They kidnapped a woman from one of them. You'll be wasting your time, gentlemen."

Schofield said, "I guess you're right. I just hate to see those damned Indians making fools of us, leading us all over the countryside and wearing our horses out. I've got a feeling we'll catch up, though, when they think they can whip us."

Healy said, "We've just got to have water tomorrow. Or we're in real trouble."

Garcia said, "The Apaches have to have water too. They'll lead us to it. Probably tomorrow."

"I sure hope you're right." The two left, threading their way back through the prostrate forms of sleeping men.

Garcia sat down and pulled off his boots. He had been watching for Shaver but the scout had not yet returned. He stretched out and closed his eyes but he did not go to sleep. He kept listening for Shaver's return even though he knew the scout might be gone all night.

He thought of Stephanie and of the woman the Apaches had taken from the little ranch they had passed yesterday. They had reached the Indians' camp at midmorning but did not find her body as he had expected. For some reason the Apaches had not killed her. Unless they had hidden her body, and that did not seem likely.

What did seem likely was that they had spared her because they wanted to give the soldiers another reason for continuing the pursuit. He lay awake for a long time, trying to think of some explanation for this apparently elaborate plan for drawing them away from the fort, for making sure they followed long after prudence dictated they should give up and return. He could think of no reason other than the long-smoldering hatred between Apaches and soldiers and that was not enough.

Shaver returned a couple of hours before daylight. He tied his horse to the picket line and hung a morral of oats over his head. Garcia, awakened by the slight sounds Shaver made, watched.

Shaver must have found water, he thought, or the scout would have watered his horse on his return. He didn't raise up and question Shaver but he'd have given considerable to know what was in Shaver's mind.

Shaver lay down to sleep the way an Apache might. He

did not even remove his boots and a couple of minutes after lying down he was snoring lustily. Shaver wasn't worried, Garcia thought, even though his horse, used more than any of the others, was certain to give out first.

That could only mean that he expected to get another one very soon. And there were only two places he could get another one. One was from some outlying ranch—a most unlikely possibility since the Apaches would already have taken whatever horses they found at ranches in their path. The other was from the Indians themselves.

Garcia suspected he was going to be able to tell when to expect the Apaches to make their attack. He'd be able to tell by carefully watching the condition of Shaver's horse.

# CHAPTER 13

When the Apaches had ridden into the first ranch in the narrow valley, Stephanie Detrick risked her own life by screaming a warning to the occupants inside the cabin. A man ran out, rifle in hand, and leveled it at the Indians, who were approaching at a hard gallop. It was the most foolish thing he could have done. There were more than twenty of the Indians. He should have slammed and barred the door and tried to fight them off from inside. Had he done so, they would have stolen his horses but they would probably have left him and the boy alive.

One of the Apaches reined his horse over and slammed him against Stephanie's. He cuffed her across the mouth with a forearm sufficiently hard to knock her tumbling from her saddle.

She got up, lips bleeding, dust in her mouth and nose, in time to see the old man go down. A boy ran from the cabin, also carrying a gun. He fired one shot before the Apaches' bullets killed him too.

Stephanie got up and ran. Away from the cabin. She had no real hope of getting away. It was just instinctive to try.

An Apache horse overtook her before she had gone fifty steps. The Indian reined the horse deliberately into her, knocking her sprawling again. When she got up this time, limping, he pointed toward the cabin and said something to her in Apache. She didn't understand his words but she understood that he meant her to return.

The man and the boy lay in front of the cabin, both dead. A couple of the Apaches had taken their guns. Now several were inside the cabin, ransacking it. Others opened the corral gate and drove the horses out. They let the horses run on down the valley, a couple of them following at a more leisurely pace.

Woodenly, Stephanie climbed on her horse. She wondered if this nightmare was ever going to end. She avoided looking at the two dead bodies but she couldn't get them out of her thoughts. They had done nothing to deserve death. They had been peaceful and harmless.

The Apaches didn't seem to resent the fact that she had screamed a warning to them. She followed down the valley, somehow grateful that they had not burned the little shack. Maybe they'd thought it would take more effort than it was worth.

At the next small cabin a woman was feeding some chickens in the yard. She saw the Indians and began to run toward the shack, but she was an old woman and couldn't run very fast. And she was nearly a hundred yards away.

The galloping Indians got ahead of her and cut her off. Her scream was cut short by a savage blow from the butt of an Indian's gun. A man came out of the shack, a rifle in his hands. He was younger than the woman, probably her son. He leveled the rifle but he never got a chance to fire it. An Apache, galloping past, leaned over and knocked him sprawling with the barrel of his gun. Before he could get up, the others riddled him.

Several of the Indians ran into the cabin to ransack it. Stephanie heard a scream, then another, and a moment later two Indians came out dragging a woman.

Stephanie had never seen such terror in a human face. Angrily she kicked her horse in the sides and rode forward. She had reached a point where she no longer cared what the Indians did to her.

Kicking out at the Indians dragging the woman along was a futile gesture but it made them halt. Surprisingly, one of them grinned. He said something to the other one.

Stephanie looked down at the woman, who was about twenty-five and would have been pretty if she had taken time to wash her face and comb her hair. She said, "It's no use to fight. There are more than twenty of them."

The woman had not noticed Stephanie until now. Hearing a voice speaking in English to her, she glanced up with sudden hope. Stephanie said, "I don't know what they intend to do to us, but they haven't killed *me* yet."

One of the Indians holding the woman pointed to Stephanie's horse and said something, plainly ordering the woman to mount behind Stephanie. The woman came to Stephanie's horse, her knees shaking so badly she could scarcely walk. She looked at her husband's body and at the old woman's and tears welled up in her eyes.

Stephanie reached a hand down and helped her mount. The woman settled on the horse's rump behind the saddle. Several Indians were driving horses out of the corral. The horses joined the bunch taken previously.

They rode on down the valley but they had not gone far before the Apaches left it to climb one of the steep ridges to the west. The woman put her arms around Stephanie's waist to keep from sliding off as the horse lunged up the slope. Stephanie held onto the saddle with all her strength.

For a while, the woman rode in stunned silence. Stephanie could feel her trembling. She wanted to say something reassuring but she didn't know what she could say.

Uneasily, she realized that the Apaches had no good reason to let this woman live. She had no value to them as a hostage.

The woman began to cry, her whole body shaking helplessly with her sobs. Stephanie turned her head. If they could talk, she thought, the woman might be less afraid. She asked, "What's your name?"

"Meg Franklin." The words came out between sobs.

"How long have you lived there? Quite a while?"

"Three years. Will said the Indians wouldn't bother us." Her weeping became hysterical as she said her husband's name.

"Was the other woman your mother? Or his?" Stephanie hated to mention the dead woman but she was running out of things to ask.

"His." The weeping subsided gradually to an occasional sob. Finally the woman asked, "Who are you? How did they get you?"

"I'm Stephanie Detrick. My husband is the commandant at Fort Lincoln. I was going there when the Indians attacked the ambulance I was riding in. They killed the four escort troopers, and the driver too."

"Do you think your husband knows? Do you think he's coming after you?"

"I don't know." Stephanie wished immediately that she'd assured Meg Franklin that the soldiers were coming to rescue them. Meg began to tremble again, as if she had a chill.

Stephanie kept talking to her, meaningless talk, anything to keep Meg's mind off what was happening. In her thoughts she was wondering bleakly if her husband was indeed following. And whether Logan Garcia was along with him.

She and Hans Detrick had lived together after their marriage for an uneasy year, with his inadequacy between them like a wall. Thinking back, she remembered how she had tried to put him at ease, to ignore what lay between them. She obviously hadn't been successful, because as soon as he could, he had obtained a transfer. First to a fort up north and then here to Fort Lincoln. She hadn't seen him since and their letters had been infrequent.

She supposed she should not have come. If she had not, perhaps those escort troopers would still be alive. Perhaps the occupants of the two ranches behind them in the little valley would also be alive.

And yet she knew her coming had been normal and natural enough. For ten years she had lived alone. Like a spinster, she thought. All her attempts to force a showdown with her husband by mail had failed. She had been left with no other alternative to coming here. Unless she wanted to live out the remainder of her life alone.

Oh God, she thought, she should have waited for Logan Garcia to return from the war. She should have had more faith. Faith that he was alive, a captive, that he would be released. But she had been too young for patience and for faith. She had believed him dead.

Now, patience and faith were a necessity. So was a lot of toughness and stamina. Of first importance was staying alive. If she did that, a chance would come to escape. When it came she must be strong enough to take advantage of it.

Puzzling to her now was the fact that the Indians seemed to have no definite destination. They seemed to be traveling almost aimlessly, not along a route that was easiest, but instead along one that seemed most difficult. She wondered if this wasn't because they knew the soldiers were following. Perhaps they were trying to wear the soldiers and their horses out.

The theory made sense. Stealing horses whenever possible, the Apaches would be able to travel farther, and faster, than the soldiers would. When the army mounts were ruined, the Apaches would be mounted on horses still able to travel.

That capturing her had been for the sole purpose of ensuring pursuit now seemed the only logical explanation for what was happening. Only that would explain the apparently aimless way the Apaches were traveling. Only that would explain the Indians' lack of haste, their failure even to try to hide their trail. Only that would explain the leaving of a scrap of petticoat impaled on the branch of a shrub at the edge of the village.

It therefore followed that the Indians must know the soldiers were close behind. By scouting back, they had determined that.

The realization brought an unexpected surge of hope. Hans was in command of the pursuing force. Logan Garcia would be with him. Of that she felt almost sure.

And even if the Indians did succeed in wearing the soldiers' horses down, that certainly didn't mean the soldiers would be easy prey.

Behind her, Meg Franklin asked, in a whispered voice, "Did they . . . did they . . . ?" She seemed unable to put her fear into words.

Stephanie shook her head. "No. They beat and kicked me until I understood that I was supposed to gather wood. But that was all." In her own heart she wasn't sure it would be the same with Meg Franklin. Meg wasn't a hostage; she was only a captive. The Indians might even want to leave her behind, dead and ravaged, as a way of reminding the cavalry what could happen to the colonel's wife.

But when they did make camp, a dry and cold camp, the

Apaches showed no interest in either of them. They were given water but no food. Two of the Apaches caught fresh mounts from among those they had stolen and rode back in the direction from which they had come. When they returned there was much talk that ended only when all the Indians lay down to sleep. Stephanie guessed the soldiers were closer than the Indians had expected them to be.

The Indians aroused the two women before daylight on the following morning by nudging them with their feet. Stephanie put a hand over Meg's mouth to stifle her scream. When the frightened woman was fully awake, she helped her up. She saddled her own horse when an Indian brought him to her. She mounted and helped Meg Franklin up.

She could gauge the condition of the cavalry horses pretty much by the condition of her own. Today it wasn't good. The horse was plainly suffering from not having anything to eat or drink last night. He faltered several times during the early part of the day, once nearly falling and sending the two women rolling down a steep and dangerous slope. But he regained his footing at the last moment, to Stephanie's vast relief.

Meg seemed much relieved today, having spent at least one safe night. But, although Stephanie didn't say anything about what she thought, she doubted if it meant anything. The Apaches had made camp late and had left their camp well before dawn. They'd had no fires and had seemed much concerned about something; she suspected they had been upset to learn that the cavalry was closer than they had believed.

The day, as hot as yesterday had been, dragged endlessly. Several times Stephanie glanced behind from the crest of some hill, hoping to see the dust of the pursuit. But she saw nothing.

The loose horses traveled a quarter mile ahead of the main body of Indians, walking no faster than they had to in the increasing heat, kept moving by two of the Indians.

That night once more they traveled until dark and made a cold, dry camp. One of the Indians gave some jerky to Stephanie and she shared it with Meg. In the morning they again broke camp before dawn and resumed their weary ride.

Finally, in the early afternoon, the group reached a small grove of cottonwood trees surrounding a wet place in the sand on the floor of a draw. While the loose horses clustered around it, the Indians got down and dug in the sand with their hands, with knives and sticks, scooping out a hole eventually that was nearly three feet deep and five or six feet across. It filled slowly with muddy water.

The Indians did not wait for it to clear. They drank, and filled their water bottles, then watered the horses they had been riding. After that, they let the loose horses gather around the water hole and drink. There was a great deal of scuffling, biting, and kicking, but eventually all the horses had the water they wanted.

Stephanie and Meg had been allowed to drink after the Indians but before the horses. Both women had cooled themselves by wetting their hair and the upper parts of their gowns.

Stephanie was glad she had no mirror with which to look at herself. She could feel the scabbed texture of her face and neck. She could see how ugly were the scabbed blisters on her hands and she knew her face was no prettier. But the shade she had fashioned had worked well and her skin hurt less than it had before. It made her feel less faint and she knew that her skin would heal.

Furthermore, the places where the saddle chafed had

ceased to pain her so terribly and were apparently beginning to toughen up. She had learned how to pad the insides of her thighs with bunched-up portions of her skirt and petticoat.

At sundown they rode down a steep slope that formed the wall of a deep canyon. Stephanie slid from the saddle, turned, and lifted Meg Franklin down. She unsaddled her horse and took the bridle off. She released the animal. Then, saying, "Come with me, no matter how bad you feel," she walked off up the narrow, dry stream bed to look for wood.

Meg looked as if she'd rather collapse, but she followed obediently, often stumbling with weariness. Stephanie loaded Meg's arms with wood before she did her own. She was terribly afraid that no matter what she did or didn't do, Meg was going to be raped and killed before they left this camp. She made up her mind that they would have to kill her too if that was what they meant to do.

Between them they carried in six loads of wood. It was, perhaps, a tribute to Stephanie that the Indians paid little attention to her, seeming to accept her almost as if she had been one of their own squaws.

Meg Franklin was different. They kept watching her, often grinning and talking among themselves as they did.

The light in the sky faded. The campfires flickered in the growing darkness. Stephanie realized that she was trembling as if she were terribly cold, even though the temperature must have been more than a hundred degrees.

She was sure Meg was saved only by the arrival of a much larger body of Indians, probably those that had been in the village they had passed through several days before. There was a lot of shouting back and forth and much activity before all the Indians—now numbering, she guessed, over two hundred—settled down to sleep.

She lay awake, staring up at the stars. Meg was safe for tonight. What bothered Stephanie now was the certainty that the battle between the Indians and the pursuing cavalry was very close.

The soldiers' horses must be in as bad a shape as her horse was, which meant the Indians must be ready. Up this canyon above the campsite, where she and Meg had gone to gather wood, the sides were so steep that no horse could climb them. When the troopers rode down into it tomorrow the Apaches would be waiting behind rocks, closing the canyon ahead of the troops, and would move in to close it behind them as soon as they had left this spot.

She didn't know what, if anything, she could do to warn the troops. She doubted if she could do anything. But she would be ready if an opportunity arose. And if it did not, then she must try to get away, taking Meg along with her. If she did not get away they both would certainly be killed, for the Indians would have no further use for them.

# CHAPTER 14

During the nearly two days since leaving the valley where the isolated ranches were, Garcia had closely watched the condition of his troop's mounts, insisting that they be unsaddled and cooled at every stop. Captains Schofield and Healy had followed his lead. It must have helped, but it had not prevented the rapid deterioration of the horses' condition as the second day progressed.

He had also watched Colonel Detrick closely, his attention drawn by Detrick's increasing nervousness. At every stop, the man paced swiftly back and forth, despite the heat. He snapped at Garcia and at others who came close to him. His hands shook.

He slept little at night, despite the exhaustion that must be as severe in him as it was in his men. Several times during the night following the discovery of the bodies at the two ranches Garcia awoke to see the colonel pacing or sitting gloomily on a rock, staring into the embers of a dying fire.

Garcia had never had much confidence in Detrick's ability. Detrick's judgments had always been erratic, not based on sober consideration but rather given hastily according to his current mood. Now he began to wonder what was going to happen when they met the enemy. Was Detrick going to go to pieces? Or would he manage to function successfully?

Apparently Schofield and Healy were worried too. For the

second time they came to him at one of the rest stops and asked, "Have you been watching the colonel?"

Garcia nodded. He didn't like these talks. They smacked of mutiny to him.

"Well, what do you think of him? Is he coming apart?"

"He's like the rest of us. He's tired and hot and irritable. That doesn't mean he's coming apart."

"That's what you're saying but it isn't what you think."

"I don't like this kind of talk. He's the commanding officer." Garcia was grateful that neither Schofield nor Healy was aware that he knew the colonel's wife.

"We don't like it either. But we know we're going to catch up with these Indians sooner or later and that when we do we're going to be in damn poor shape to fight. We need a commander who's got his wits about him."

"Detrick will do all right." Garcia's voice was curt. Such discussions could have no useful purpose and they would inevitably undermine the effectiveness of the captains who indulged in them even if they did not result in open mutiny.

The two left him, grumbling. The column went on, still following the plain trail left by the Indians.

The trail had tended south now for at least two days. Garcia felt fairly certain they could not be more than a few miles from the Mexican border. He was also reasonably sure Detrick intended to ignore the border, even if he knew when they came to it.

The afternoon dragged. Rest stops were both longer and more frequent now. The pace had slowed. Yet in spite of their slower progress, Hiram Shaver reported the trail to be fresher, no more than four hours old.

The men were too tired and listless to fight among themselves anymore. Garcia had the uneasy realization that, even if they were to turn back to the fort right now, they would not make it without losses to both horses and men.

Toward evening they rode into a shallow draw and discovered a few stunted cottonwood trees surrounding a dugout water hole where the Apaches had obviously stopped during the afternoon.

Sight of water immediately picked the men's spirits up. They took turns lying down around the water hole and drinking their fill. They splashed water onto their faces and over themselves. When all the men had drunk their fill, when all water casks had been refilled and all canteens, then the horses were permitted access to the water hole.

Tonight even more than previously, Garcia kept his eye on Shaver, because he had a feeling in his guts that the battle with the Apaches was very near. As he expected, Shaver rode out at sundown to scout.

Without consulting Detrick, who seemed numb and preoccupied, Garcia beckoned Hazelthorne. The two got their horses from the troop's picket line, which was around a bend in the draw and out of the colonel's view, and mounted them. Garcia picked up Shaver's trail and followed it, with Hazelthorne close behind.

The trail followed the Indians' trail. Shaver was apparently riding at a steady trot. Up over the edge of the draw went the trail. At the top, Garcia halted and stared back at the three troops bivouacked below. Again he had the feeling that their battle with the Indians was very near.

The two rode on up the low ridge, dropping behind its crest so as not to be visible to anyone who might be looking up toward them. The light gradually faded from the sky, which was cloudless and, before gray began to dim its color, almost like brass. Darker and darker it became until finally

Garcia had to dismount and bend close to the ground in order to see the scout's trail.

Eventually it became impossible to see the trail at all any longer. Hazelthorne asked in a whisper, "What are you goin' to do now, sir?"

Garcia led his horse off thirty yards or so from the trail. He said, "I guess we wait."

"What do you think Shaver's doin', sir?"

"I think he's meeting the Indians."

Hazelthorne did not reply. They waited, as silently as they could, for more than an hour. Finally Garcia whispered, "I guess we'd just as well go back."

He was mounting when Hazelthorne whispered urgently, "Wait a minute, sir."

Garcia froze. Listening intently, he heard the scuff of an approaching horse's hoofs. He swung himself to the saddle, hitting it silently. Hazelthorne followed suit.

Garcia waited until the approaching horse was nearly abreast. Then he dug spurs into his horse's sides. The animal leaped obediently ahead.

He had thought the horseman was Shaver and was only prepared to take the man by surprise, hoping to startle him enough to cause him to let something slip. As he closed with the rider, he was himself startled to discover it was not Shaver but an Indian.

Having discovered that, he reacted instantly. Savagely his spurs raked his horse's sides again and as the animal leaped forward, he reined him straight into the Indian's horse. As the two collided, Garcia left his saddle, encircling the Apache's neck with one arm.

His momentum carried both him and the Apache on beyond both horses and they tumbled to the ground. It was dark and there was no time to bring weapons into play. Garcia tightened his throttle hold on the Apache's throat, knowing he had cut the man's air supply.

For a time, the Apache tried frantically to loosen Garcia's grip. He failed, no matter how violently his body thrashed. Apparently knowing if he did not do something else immediately he was going to lose consciousness, the Apache abandoned his efforts to pry Garcia's arms loose and his hand groped for the knife at his side.

Garcia realized instantly what was in the Indian's mind. With one arm still cutting off the Indian's air, he grabbed for the Apache's knife hand with the other.

He was too late. The knife came free of its scabbard and raked him lengthwise along the thigh. Having lost his advantage and been wounded too, Garcia now released the Indian's throat and groped for the savage's knife hand with both his own.

The Indian now was choking, gasping, trying to draw breath into his lungs. Garcia got hold of his knife wrist with both hands and twisted savagely, causing the knife to drop to the ground.

For an instant they were separated by a distance of a couple of feet. Hazelthorne, waiting carbine in hand, took advantage of the opportunity. Brutally he struck downward with the butt of his carbine. The sound of it striking the Indian's head was solid, crunching, and final. The Indian slumped.

Garcia struggled to his feet. He didn't know how bad the thigh wound was but he could feel the warm wetness of blood running down his leg. He said shortly, "Thanks."

"You think he's the only one, sir?"

"Probably. Let's get started back."

"What are we goin' to do with him?"

"Drag him off to the side of the trail. But bring his horse along."

He fumbled in his pocket for a match, struck it, and looked at the wound in his leg. It burned now. It was about ten inches long and maybe a quarter inch deep. It was bleeding profusely but it wasn't going to incapacitate him. He mounted his horse.

Hazelthorne caught the Indian's horse, mounted his own, and followed Garcia back toward camp. Garcia held his horse to a walk despite his anxiety to get his leg tied up, knowing how near exhaustion was his horse.

It must have been near ten o'clock when they rode down the slope into the bivouac. Detrick was pacing back and forth beside a dying fire. He scowled at Garcia and Hazelthorne and snapped, "Where the hell have you two been?"

Garcia said, "We followed Shaver. He got away from us but we caught ourselves an Indian."

Detrick glanced quickly at the Indian's horse. "Where is he?"

"Dead." Garcia gestured toward his leg. Turning his head, he said to Hazelthorne, "See if you can round up some bandages out of one of the mule packs, Sergeant." Hazelthorne left. Garcia said, "Colonel, I believe Shaver is making contact with the Indians. He probably missed tonight for some reason and that's why we ran into the Indian."

"That's ridiculous."

"Maybe. Is he back yet?"

"No." For the first time, Detrick's expression was uncertain.

"Sir, I've got an idea." He hesitated. He had been about

to ask that the colonel let him take his troop, make a forced night march, and attack the Indian camp at dawn.

Just in time, he realized that was not a diplomatic approach. He said, "Colonel, why don't you take my troop, make a night march, and hit that Indian camp at dawn? We can pick the strongest horses. Maybe if we hit them when they don't expect it we can get this thing over with and rescue your wife at the same time. They're going to kill her if we don't catch them by surprise."

Detrick started to shake his head. He was scowling but he was also hesitating. Probably, thought Garcia, he also was beginning to suspect Shaver. Garcia said softly, "Colonel, we're not gaining on these Indians. I think they're just leading us around until we can't travel anymore."

"There are only about twenty of them."

"Yes, sir. Twenty now. But there were a hundred and fifty wickiups in the village we went through. That adds up to more than two hundred fighting men."

The tempo of the colonel's pacing increased. Studying his face, Garcia could see how badly he wanted to refuse. He didn't want suggestions from Garcia. He didn't want his wife's rescue, if it was accomplished, to be due to a suggestion from Garcia.

But he also knew how near exhaustion were the horses of his command, to say nothing of the men themselves. While he was hesitating, both men heard a horse coming down the slope. Shaver rode into camp.

Detrick stared suspiciously at him. "Where have you been all this time?"

Shaver was looking at the Indian horse. "Where did he come from?"

"Captain Garcia and Hazelthorne surprised an Indian."

Shaver's glance switched instantly to Garcia. There was anger in his eyes but he didn't say anything.

Detrick said, "I am going to take Captain Garcia's troop and the strongest of the horses and make a forced night march. We will attack the Indians at dawn."

Shaver almost instantly turned his face away but not before Garcia had seen the sudden alarm it showed. That expression confirmed every suspicion he'd ever had about the scout. He said, "You will not leave camp, Mr. Shaver, until we are ready to leave."

Shaver did not turn around. Garcia said, "I'll rouse the men, Colonel."

"Yes, Captain. Do that. I will keep an eye on Mr. Shaver while you're gone."

Hazelthorne approached with some bandages. Garcia gave him the order to rouse the men of C Troop and to select the strongest horses for them to ride. Shaver had said today that the Indians were four hours ahead. If they left within the hour, they could reach the Indian camp before first light.

# CHAPTER 15

Detrick watched Garcia rip his trousers away from the knife wound on his thigh, watched him wind bandages around the leg. Finished, Garcia left, probably to get a fresh pair of trousers.

Detrick's own suspicions of Shaver had been increasing during the past few days. It seemed that only when the column desperately needed water to keep going did they find it. Furthermore, the Indians' failure to hide their trail was suspicious. It was apparent that the Indians wanted to be followed and that could lead to only one conclusion. As Garcia had predicted, an ambush would be waiting for the three troops of cavalry someplace ahead.

When that time came, the Apaches would have no further use for Stephanie. The prospect of her death, while it was not something he wanted, had continued to stir speculation in Detrick's mind. With Stephanie dead, his problem would disappear. The confrontation she had come out here for would not have to take place. He would be spared a lot of humiliation and embarrassment.

He didn't like himself very much when he had such thoughts. But he couldn't help having them.

He also continued to consider the possibility that Garcia might be killed in the coming fight. If both Garcia and Stephanie were killed, there would be no physical reminders of his inadequacy left and maybe he could forget.

Subconsciously he might wish both of them dead. But consciously he knew he would never do anything to bring about that end. He could never kill Garcia himself, even in the heat of battle. He could never do anything that would ensure Stephanie's death at the hands of the Indians. He had his failings but he was basically a decent man.

Shaver stood, scowling, at the edge of the fire. Detrick picked up a couple of sticks and threw them on, wanting more light with which to study Shaver's face.

Shaver kept fidgeting. Detrick asked, "What's the matter, Mr. Shaver?"

"Matter?"

"You seem pretty nervous."

"It's because we're so damn close to the Mexican border, Colonel. I don't know exactly where it is and I don't want you to get into trouble on account of me."

"And that's all you're worrying about?"

"Colonel, if you run into Mexican troops . . . well, it's something to worry about."

"Those savages have my wife. I'll chase them into hell if that's what it takes." Brave words, he thought. After a moment, he asked, "What makes you think we're so close to the border?"

"There's a deep drainage just short of the border called Soda Creek. I thought I saw it before it got dark."

"You can stop worrying, Mr. Shaver. The responsibility is mine, not yours."

Shaver nodded. He started to turn away. Detrick said quickly, "Stay right where you are, Mr. Shaver. We'll be moving out before very long."

"Is that an order, Colonel?"

"Yes, Mr. Shaver. That's exactly what it is."

Shaver stared at him speculatively. Finally, with the faintest of shrugs, he turned back to the fire.

Detrick was glad his inner uncertainty hadn't been apparent to the scout. He didn't know what he would have done if Shaver had deliberately disobeyed. He was still not completely convinced that Garcia's accusation had been true. Doubting, he wasn't sure he could have shot Shaver. But apparently Shaver had been uncertain enough to prevent him from taking the chance. If he was a traitor, as Garcia suspected, he'd try getting away to warn the Indians sometime during the night march. If he was not, there was nothing to worry about.

Detrick could hear the sounds of C Troop being awakened, rising, going to get their mounts. There was an occasional, muted shout. The other two troops could come up tomorrow, he thought, as reserves. If by then things weren't going well, their arrival should turn things around.

But there was really no reason why things should not go well. Only twenty or so Indians were up ahead of them. A troop of cavalry, with surprise on its side, should make quick work of that many Indians.

Then why did he feel so much uneasiness? He examined his own feelings for an answer.

The truth was, he didn't have any experience at this sort of thing. During the war, he'd had an administrative post with General Sherman's staff. The closest he had come to the fighting was the distant sound of cannon fire and once the crackling of muskets in the woods.

Up north, he'd never had occasion to fight any Indians. Down here at Fort Lincoln, the only action he'd seen was the Arroyo Blanco attack, when a small village of Apaches had been taken by surprise, and an occasional exchange of a few shots with a handful of Indians encountered on patrol.

This was different. At least twenty seasoned Apache warriors were ahead of them. If what Garcia suspected was true, there could be more. He realized that his hands were shaking and he clasped them in back of him.

"Hell," he thought, "I'm a soldier. I'm in command of all these men." And anyway, he wasn't actually afraid. He was just unsure of himself. He was more afraid of making a disastrous mistake than he was of being shot. That was what was behind his nervousness.

He consoled himself that every commander probably felt this way before a battle. It was perfectly normal. When the shooting began, he would be as cool as a seasoned officer. If he wasn't . . . well, by God, nobody was going to know.

He stared across the fire at Hiram Shaver. His eyes met those of the scout and for an instant he thought Shaver was going to try to walk away. He told himself that if Shaver did, he would shoot him in the back. He would call out once and then would shoot.

Shaver saw that determination in his eyes. He frowned and lowered his glance to the fire, thinking that he had all night to get away. He didn't have to do anything foolish now.

Private Hutchcroft watched as Sergeant Hazelthorne and a couple of other men walked along the picket lines, selecting the strongest of the mounts. He accepted the one assigned to him and led the animal to where his saddle was. He threw on the saddle blanket, smoothed it out, then threw up the McClellan saddle and cinched it tight.

There was a fierce excitement in him. At last, after all this waiting, he was going to get his revenge. He promised himself that he would kill an Apache for every member of his fiancée's family. That was the minimum. And two for her.

That wasn't going to even the score, of course. But it would be a start. He checked his ammunition belt, checked the load in his carbine. He was ready. He was like a hound, straining at the leash and ready to take the trail.

Private Jenkins faced the night and the dawn attack with dread. He accepted and saddled the mount assigned to him with hands that shook violently. A dozen feet from Hutchcroft, he saw the man check his ammunition belt and his carbine's load. Following suit, he checked his own.

He wondered if everyone going into battle for the first time felt like this. Certainly Hutchcroft did not, but Hutchcroft was different. He had been waiting for this opportunity ever since his promised wife and her family had been murdered by the Indians. If he felt any fear, which Jenkins doubted, it was submerged beneath his nearly fanatical thirst for revenge.

He couldn't stand doing nothing so he meticulously checked every item of his gear. He checked his horse's shoes. Around him, others of C Troop were saddling. The men of the other troops had been awakened by the commotion, but most of them stayed where they were, trying to sleep in spite of the noise.

Detrick sent his orderly with a message to the other troop officers to join him immediately. They came walking toward the colonel's fire, saluted, and waited for what he had to say. There were Captain Healy and Lieutenant Ben Harris of K Troop, and Captain Schofield and Lieutenant Robert LeRoy Poole of B. Garcia joined them and so did Scott Martell, C Troop's lieutenant.

From where he stood, Jenkins could hear everything the colonel said. "I'm taking C Troop on a night march to try and surprise these Indians, who Shaver says are no more than four hours ahead of us. You men will move out no later than first light as reserves. If we have no more than the twenty or so Indians we have been following to contend with, there should be no need for you. But Captain Garcia thinks we may encounter a larger number, the men from the abandoned village we passed through. I want you to reconnoiter the battle, if one is going on, before plunging in."

There was a murmur among the junior officers. Detrick said, "That's all, then. Return to your commands. One more thing—leave the pack train behind. Leave half a dozen men with it as guards."

The captains and lieutenants left the fire and returned to their commands. Detrick said, "All right, Captain Garcia. Form your troop."

Garcia shouted to Hazelthorne, whose roar rolled out over the bivouac. Men mounted their horses. They milled with apparent disorganization but in five minutes the troop stood facing Detrick's fire in a long, uneven line.

There was little fidgeting among the mounts, tired from the days that were behind. Garcia stared at his troop, measuring the nervousness among the men and glad that it was there. Nervousness and even fear had its place because it took away the men's weariness.

More closely, he studied the horses. They were, he guessed, good for four more hours if they weren't ridden recklessly. And the chances were good that whatever fighting was done tomorrow at dawn would be done on foot.

Detrick's orderly brought his horse. Corporal Delaney brought Garcia's horse to him. The captain swung to the saddle.

Shaver had changed the saddle from his own weary horse to the back of the captured Indian horse. He mounted and waited.

Watching him, Garcia made up his mind that if he

watched nothing else during the next four hours he was going to watch the scout. He felt certain Shaver would, at some time during the night, try to slip away and warn the Indians.

And if they were warned, there would be no remaining hope of rescuing Stephanie Detrick alive. The Indians would kill her before the attack took place.

Detrick and Shaver rode at the column's head. Garcia and Hazelthorne rode a dozen yards behind. Behind came C Troop, silent, with each man thinking his own private thoughts.

# CHAPTER 16

Stephanie Detrick lay awake for a long, long time. She tried to go to sleep but it was impossible. For a while she thought the reason was that she was simply too tired, that her body hurt too much to permit her to sleep. Gradually, however, she became aware that physical discomfort was not the reason at all. The real reason was uneasiness.

Gathering wood up the dry gulch away from the Indians' camp, she had seen the way the canyon narrowed, the way the slopes steepened until finally, a quarter mile above the camp, they were so steep that only a mountain goat could have climbed out of the canyon. Certainly no horse could negotiate those slopes.

But Apaches could, on foot. And she realized that was exactly what they planned. The entire body of Apache warriors were now gathered here. They were well armed and had plenty of ammunition. Tomorrow morning they would disperse to right and left, climb the canyon slopes, and take up concealed positions behind rocks and clumps of brush.

Others would drive the horses on up the canyon, thus ensuring pursuit by the troops. When the soldiers were strung out in the narrow defile, the Apaches would open fire from their concealed positions in the rocks. It would be a massacre. There was probably not a single place above this camp where a horse could negotiate the slopes. Which meant the troops would have to turn and try to get back to this spot.

And Stephanie felt sure the Apaches would have massed their best marksmen here to prevent the troops from doing so. Horses and men would pile up in the narrow canyon floor. If a single man escaped, it would be a miracle.

Furthermore, if she and Meg were not killed first thing in the morning it would only mean the Apaches were saving them for the victory celebration after the fight.

The Apaches' plan was flawless so far as Stephanie could see, although she admitted to being less than a military strategist.

Her mind was like an animal in a cage, darting back and forth, seeking a way out, not only for Meg and herself, but for the troops who would arrive at this place sometime tomorrow. She could find no way. She could see no possibility of escape, either for Meg or herself. And she remembered the way the Indians who had joined their captors earlier had looked at them, some of them making obscene gestures, a few even touching Meg and pulling at her clothes until they were stopped by an older Indian with an air of authority.

All night Stephanie lay awake, desperately searching for a plan. The truth was, there simply wasn't any plan that had a chance to work. This scheme had been planned too well. It was foolproof and it was going to work.

Hiram Shaver, riding beside Colonel Detrick and staring broodily into the night, felt a desperation he could hardly control. He had not expected the soldiers to undertake a forced night march. Not considering the condition of their mounts. He had not planned for it and neither had the Indians. They were asleep right now in the canyon of Soda Creek, confident that the soldiers were four hours away. It was doubtful if they had even posted guards.

And there was no reason, he told himself angrily, why he

should have expected such a development. The men of these three troops were near exhaustion and their horses were in worse shape than they. It was questionable whether the horses could make it back to Fort Lincoln even if they turned around and started back tomorrow.

So a forced night march after a long day of traveling in the blistering heat had simply been unthinkable. But it was going to take place. And unless he did something and warned the Indians, the whole careful plan he had formulated with Manuelito might fail.

Tonight he had missed making contact with the Apache sent back to meet him. He didn't know how he had missed. He had stayed on the trail but maybe the Indian had not. In any case, Garcia and Hazelthorne had encountered the Indian and had killed him. But even if Shaver had contacted the Indian it would have made no difference. He hadn't known about the night march at the time.

Riding along now beside Colonel Detrick, he told himself he shouldn't be worrying. This troop, even including its noncoms and officers, numbered barely over fifty men. The Apaches had more than two hundred in the Soda Creek defile. Yet he knew that if C Troop managed to hit the sleeping Indian camp at dawn, completely surprising them, the Apaches might go down in defeat. A lot of them would undoubtedly escape. But his carefully formulated plan would fail. He would achieve no revenge against Detrick and his troops for the death of his wife and sons. It was even possible that, in the confusion, Detrick would manage to rescue his wife alive.

The thought was maddening to Shaver, who had been kept going by this plan for many months. He had to get away. He had to reach the Indian camp, rouse them, and set the ambush up. Whatever the risk, he had to get away.

Because if this troop hit the Indian camp at dawn and killed many Indians, Shaver's ties with the Indians would be gone. He would never be able to return to the Apache villages. They would believe him guilty of treachery.

Neither could he stay among the whites. He would be brought to trial for treachery and probably sent to prison. And even if he was not convicted, he would be branded forever as a traitor to his own kind. There would be no place he could go.

Only in one way could he salvage anything. That was by escaping and reaching the Indians. But hell, he ought to be able to do that all right. He wasn't tied. He had this Indian horse under him, probably a stronger horse than any being ridden by the cavalrymen. They probably couldn't catch him if he could get a start of fifty yards.

That fifty yards was the crucial thing. There was a half moon almost directly overhead and it gave enough light for pretty good shooting up to fifty yards. The instant he broke away, they'd open up on him. And they'd get him, too, unless he managed to reach cover immediately.

He would have to wait, therefore, for a spot where there was either a lot of cover or a ravine. Trying to appear sleepy, he let his head sag forward and let his shoulders slump. But his eyes ceaselessly searched the terrain ahead.

Garcia and Hazelthorne rode about fifty feet behind Shaver and the colonel. Garcia knew Shaver was going to try getting away and he conceded that there was a chance he could succeed. Detrick wouldn't be able to catch him and probably wouldn't even try. If Detrick got off a single shot, that was about the most that could be expected of him.

Furthermore, he and Hazelthorne, riding fifty feet behind, would have little chance of catching Shaver in the dark. Shaver was sure to wait for a place where there was scrub timber or brush. Or else he would wait for a draw or ridge where the terrain itself would hide him for the first precious few seconds when he would either make good his escape or fail.

Softly, Garcia said, "That son-of-a-bitch is going to get away. And if he does, the Indians are going to be waiting for us." In the soft moonlight he could dimly make out dark patches of undergrowth ahead. He hesitated a moment and finally said, "I'm going to ride off down the ridge to the left. When I get a chance, I'll get ahead of Shaver and Detrick. I can keep position by listening to the sounds made by the men, but I won't have any way of knowing when Shaver makes his break. I want you to keep your gun handy. When he bolts, you fire."

"Yes, sir." Hazelthorne shifted his carbine so that his right hand was on the receiver, his finger through the trigger guard. He eased the hammer back to full cock.

Garcia guided his horse off the trail to the left. There was little difficulty in doing so here because the top of the ridge along which they were riding was wide and gently rounded. Later it might be different but he'd face that possibility when it arose.

He put about fifty yards between himself and the column, and then, by trotting his horse, managed to forge ahead shielded by the undergrowth. Only when he was fifty yards ahead of Detrick and Shaver did he slow his horse to a walk again. He hoped Detrick didn't look around and discover that he was gone, but he supposed Hazelthorne would think up some explanation for his absence if the colonel did.

He also hoped Shaver's ears didn't pick up the sounds of his horse. But there was a slight breeze blowing toward him from the top of the ridge and that would help keep sounds from reaching Shaver's ears.

Half an hour passed. The ridge began to descend, and suddenly Garcia found himself riding through very heavy brush. The noise made by his horse increased. Uneasily he glanced in the colonel's direction, worrying about being heard.

The gunshot made him start violently because he had been thinking mostly about the noise he was making riding in the heavy brush. But he reacted instantly, stiffening, digging spurs into his horse's sides. Recklessly he swung hard over and took a course forty-five degrees right of the one he had been following.

He heard Colonel Detrick shout. Another gun roared and then suddenly, directly ahead of him, his ears picked up the sounds of a horse crashing through the heavy brush. In the moonlight he glimpsed a dark shadow beneath which were splotches of white. The pinto Indian pony, he knew, with Shaver riding it, was less than twenty-five yards ahead.

Fully aware that Shaver's horse was stronger than his own, he raked his horse's sides savagely with his spurs and beat the startled animal across the rump with his pistol barrel. The animal forgot for the moment how tired he was. His long legs reached out and he began to gain rapidly on Shaver's horse.

Until now, Shaver had not heard him but suddenly he did. Hipping around in his saddle, he fired twice at Garcia, missing both times because of the way his horse was lunging through the brush.

Garcia's revolver was in his hand but he made no attempt to fire it. Either he would catch Shaver or he would not. If he failed to catch the man he was going to need every bullet that was in his gun.

He let out a sudden, shrill yell, further startling his horse. Now he could see that the distance between him and Shaver was closing rapidly. The heart of the thoroughbred Garcia was riding showed in the way the gallant animal gave everything he had in one sudden, short burst of speed. His head drew abreast of the rump of Shaver's horse.

Once more, Shaver hipped around in his saddle, raised and leveled his gun. Garcia knew the scout couldn't miss this time. The gun muzzle was no more than six feet away from him.

Without hesitation, he raised his own gun, thumbed the hammer back, and fired in a motion that was unbelievably swift and continuous. Both guns roared almost simultaneously.

As he fired, Garcia threw himself forward over the withers of his horse. Shaver's bullet, aimed at his chest, raked the muscles of his back instead, burning like a branding iron.

Shaver, catching Garcia's bullet squarely in the throat, tumbled from his saddle, but not before he sprayed Garcia liberally with his gushing blood. Garcia hauled his horse to a halt.

Shaver's horse, the Indian pony, stood trembling for an instant. Then he broke into a run again, straight ahead toward the Indian camp. Garcia raised his gun a second time and fired swiftly at the horse's rapidly disappearing shape. His bullet struck and the horse went crashing down.

Behind Garcia, the colonel appeared. With the colonel was Hazelthorne and close behind the two was the head of the column. Garcia dismounted. His back was burning like fire but he had no intention of stopping the column while it was taken care of. Detrick asked, "How the hell did you manage to catch him so fast?"

Garcia realized that Detrick didn't know he had been riding ahead of the column waiting for Shaver to try getting away. He saw no reason to tell the colonel that. He said, "I guess this horse is just a damn good animal, Colonel. At least for a short sprint. If I hadn't caught him when I did, though, he'd have gotten clean away."

Detrick said, "All right, let's get out of here. The other troops can bury him when they find him tomorrow."

He led out, now with both Garcia and Hazelthorne riding beside him where Shaver had been before.

No longer could there be doubt that Shaver had planned everything that was happening, from the kidnapping of Stephanie Detrick to the ambush that waited for them up ahead.

What now remained was to try and salvage something out of what would have been a complete disaster if they had not decided to make this forced night march.

# CHAPTER 17

Fortunately the trail left by the Indians was still as plain as before and, even in the light of the half moon, was easily followed. Also fortunately for the horses, the night air was fairly cool, probably no more than ninety degrees.

Detrick still did not understand how Garcia had managed to overtake Shaver so quickly. Garcia had been riding fifty feet behind. He remembered now that he hadn't seen Garcia go past but, he decided, that wasn't too surprising. He'd been taken by surprise when Shaver bolted. He'd been busy getting his gun clear of its holster and trying to decide whether he would shoot Shaver in the back or not. Garcia could have gone past unnoticed while he was thus preoccupied.

Once again, he thought resentfully, he had come out looking ineffectual and indecisive and Garcia had, as always, come out of it looking like a hero. It would probably be the same when they encountered the Indians at dawn.

The trail began to climb and, every half hour or so, it was necessary to stop and let the horses rest. As usual, Garcia made his men remove their saddles and cool their horses' backs. Detrick struck a match and looked at his watch. They had been traveling nearly three hours. There was only about an hour and a half left before first light. Detrick began to feel a sense of urgency. If they were late getting to the Indian camp and arrived after daylight, this could turn from a

surprise attack into a disaster. Particularly if by now the
score or so of Indians they had been following had been
reinforced.

Finally, when only an hour of darkness remained, Garcia
pointed ahead. Detrick could see, in the cold light of the
moon now lying low in the western sky, a gash in the nearly
level high plateau that stretched away to right and left for
as far as the eye could see. From here it didn't look very
wide, but Detrick knew that was illusion caused by distance
and by the angle at which they were viewing it.

Garcia said, "Colonel, I'd like permission to go ahead. My
guess is that they're camped in that canyon. Maybe I can
get close enough to tell if they've been reinforced."

Detrick hesitated a moment. He knew he needed the information Garcia proposed to get. If he'd had anyone else as
capable as Garcia he'd have sent him instead. But he did
not. And if whoever went ahead to scout gave his presence
away, all chance of surprise would be gone. He nodded re-
luctantly. "All right. Go ahead."

Garcia said, "I'd like to take Sergeant Hazelthorne."

Again Detrick hesitated. He thought he knew why Garcia
wanted Hazelthorne. Garcia wanted to be free to go in and
try rescuing Stephanie if it looked to him as if there was any
chance of doing it. He wanted Hazelthorne along so he
could send him back with whatever information he had obtained. But Detrick said, "All right."

Garcia and Hazelthorne kicked their weary mounts into a
trot. They disappeared into the darkness ahead.

Holding their horses to a steady trot, Garcia and
Hazelthorne reached the rim of the canyon in about twenty
minutes. Well short of it, both men dismounted and tied
their horses to stout clumps of brush. On foot and walking
quietly, they continued to the canyon rim.

The canyon was half a mile wide here at the top. Its sides were steep, but this was where the Indians had gone down into it, so Garcia knew it was passable for a horse.

Moving quickly but quietly, trying to ignore the growing stiffness in his leg and back, he went along the canyon rim to the right for a couple of hundred yards. From a promontory here he could see how it narrowed and how much steeper were its sides. No horse could climb out of the canyon above the place where he had left Hazelthorne. And he began to see the diabolic efficiency with which the Indians had planned this ambush for the three troops of cavalry.

They would have been gone by the time the troops arrived tomorrow. Their trail would have gone up the canyon floor and the troopers would have followed it, with Detrick reasoning that if the Indians headed up the canyon there had to be a way out someplace. Only there probably wasn't a way out, at least not one that a horse could negotiate. The Indians would be waiting behind rocks on the canyon's sides. They'd have cut the soldiers to pieces with little risk to themselves because they'd have been well covered, the troopers pitilessly exposed.

He returned to Hazelthorne. Beckoning, he led Hazelthorne down the canyon for several hundred yards, moving at a trot, conscious of the way time was slipping away.

From another promontory he could see the way the canyon widened in this direction. About half a mile away he could see a little draw feeding into the canyon that would make an easy trail to reach the canyon floor.

He led Hazelthorne back to their original vantage point. The canyon floor was in shadow and he couldn't see anything, neither the shapes of men nor horses, so he couldn't tell whether the Indians had been reinforced or not. He could, however, see the glow from several dying fires, more than twenty Indians normally would have.

He said, "Ride back and meet the colonel. Tell him about that little draw down the canyon and tell him I suggest that he send ten men down it to the canyon floor. They're to move in toward the Indian camp quietly and take up positions behind rocks so that they can cover that route of escape.

"Tell him to send another ten men upcountry half a mile with instructions to work their way down the canyon slope on foot until they're within accurate rifle range of the bottom. They can keep the Indians from escaping that way."

Hazelthorne said, "Where will you be, sir?"

"Never mind that. Tell the colonel that when those two groups are in position, he can take the remainder of the troop down into the canyon here. I figure the Indians will either go up the canyon or down instead of standing and fighting the force coming at them from here. Either way they go, they'll run into an ambush. But by the time they do, the colonel will be safely on the canyon floor."

"I'll tell him. But he's going to want to know where you are, sir. What am I going to tell him?"

"Tell him I'm going into the Apache camp and try to get his wife."

"Captain, that's suicide."

"I'm not going to commit suicide, Hazelthorne. I'm not going to get caught."

"No, sir."

"Get going then. Can you remember everything I said?"

"Yes, sir. I'll remember."

"It's getting late. Don't waste any time."

Hazelthorne disappeared into the darkness. Garcia left his horse tied. Moving slowly and carefully, he began the descent to the canyon floor on foot. He tested each step before putting his weight down, knowing that a single rock dislodged by a foot and tumbling to the bottom would alert the Apaches to his presence and not only cost him his life but probably spoil Detrick's chance of surprising the Indian camp at dawn.

Thinking about Detrick, he had a moment when he wished somebody else was in command of C Troop. Almost anyone. Maybe Detrick would heed the advice he had sent back with Hazelthorne and maybe he would not. Garcia had sensed Detrick's resentment toward him. So far that resentment hadn't caused Detrick to go against his better judgment as an officer. That didn't mean it wouldn't. And if Detrick failed to carry out the strategy Garcia had suggested, then the whole engagement was likely to turn into a debacle.

Essentially what Garcia had proposed was, he felt certain, what the Indians had planned for the cavalry. Closing off the way ahead and the way back, stationing riflemen behind rocks on the slopes to cut the trapped cavalrymen down.

But why? He had no answer for that question, even though he knew there had to have been a reason and a powerful one.

Step by careful step, he continued to work his way down the steep and rocky slope. He could now see the forms of sleeping men. He could hear the movement of the horse herd, being held farther up the canyon. And he realized that this camp below him contained many times the number of Indians they had been following. Making a rough count at one of his rest stops, he decided there must be more than two hundred Apaches on the canyon floor. Uneasily, he realized that fact might make it impossible for C Troop to drive them anywhere.

He paused often now, squatting silently whenever he did,

searching the darkness for the form of an Indian guard. He saw none and began to wonder if it was possible they had put out no guards.

Knowing they had a spy in the soldiers' camp, he supposed it was possible. They thought the soldiers were at least four hours away. They probably had not even considered the possibility of a night march by the troops.

He went on. He was now less than a hundred yards from the bottom of the slope. He began looking for a place to hide himself, a place that would give him some cover if he happened to be discovered.

Such a place was a huge rock off to his right about fifty yards. It had apparently broken off from the rim in ages past, tumbled most of the way to the bottom, and, for some reason, stopped before reaching it. It was about four feet square and would afford him a perfect hiding place.

Carefully, he eased toward it. Watching both the rock and the sleeping Indians less than a hundred yards away from him, he was, for an instant, less careful than he should have been about the ground underfoot. His foot dislodged a rock and it bounded down the slope.

Instantly Garcia froze. He hunched down, hugging his knees with his arms. The rock bounded to the bottom, in the predawn silence sounding to Garcia like an avalanche.

Several Indians raised up. A couple got to their feet and stared toward the slope where Garcia was. Silently, he thanked God that the setting moon had put the canyon floor in shadow. Motionless he squatted there, scarcely daring to breathe, knowing any movement he made would be spotted instantly. His only hope lay in the probability that his dark hunched shape would be mistaken for a rock.

A couple of voices called out in Apache, the words guttural and making no sense to him. He let his glance rove from one end of the camp to the other, looking for Stephanie and the woman the Apaches had kidnapped from the small ranch, but it was still too dark to make anything out definitely.

Finally, those Indians who had raised up, settled back again. One of those who was on his feet added a few sticks of wood to one of the fires. He stood before the growing blaze, staring down into it.

Garcia wished he'd been able to reach the rock but he didn't dare try getting to it now. A dozen or more Indians, wakened by the stone he had dislodged, were probably still watching the slope. He'd have to wait. And very little time remained before gray began to lighten up the sky.

The canyon floor would, of course, grow light later than would the plateau above. Garcia caught himself listening intently for any little sound from above that would tell him Detrick and C Troop had arrived. He heard nothing no matter how he strained his ears.

It began to look as if the Indian by the fire wasn't going back to sleep. Silently Garcia cursed his own carelessness in dislodging that single rock. He shifted his position so that his carbine was across his chest, ready to fire at an instant's notice.

It wouldn't take much light to make him visible on this slope. His tunic was blue and even in faint first light would stand out sharply against the dun-colored rocks on the slope.

With growing desperation he searched the sleeping forms on the valley floor. Here, alone, with two hundred Apaches a hundred yards away, he admitted he had little or no chance of rescuing either woman. He had practically no chance of surviving himself. He had been a fool to come. But if he had not come both Stephanie and the other woman would have died immediately after the first volley of shots rang out.

He finally saw a spot of something that looked lighter than the other sleeping forms. He squinted, straining his eyes, trying to decide definitely what it was, but he could not.

The man at the fire had turned and now had his back toward Garcia on the slope. Carefully, with infinite slowness, Garcia eased himself up into a half crouch. Testing each footfall, he sidled along the slope toward the shelter of the rock.

The man at the fire turned and Garcia froze. The man looked at the slope for several moments before he looked away again.

Now the compulsion to sprint for the shelter of the rock was almost irresistible. But Garcia successfully resisted it. Once more, a cautious step at a time, he eased toward the rock.

When he finally reached it, he was bathed with sweat. He knelt, trembling, and leaned his carbine against the rock. He had made it. For the time being he was safe. But he still had to locate the two women and figure out some way to save their lives.

# CHAPTER 18

Colonel Detrick reached the canyon rim about half an hour before dawn. The moon now hung low in the western sky, casting long shadows on the ground. Detrick halted C Troop a couple of hundred yards short of the rim and rode forward with Lieutenant Martell and Sergeant Hazelthorne to look down. Softly he spoke to Hazelthorne. "Is this the place?"

"Yes, sir."

Detrick stared into the void, unable to see the bottom, unable to see the slope more than fifty yards below the rim. He asked, "Are you sure we can get down this way? It looks pretty steep to me. I'd hate to get caught halfway down and not be able to get either up or down."

Hazelthorne tried to see the colonel's face in the darkness. That tone of uncertainty in his commanding officer made him uneasy. He said, "Colonel, this is the way the Apaches went down. If they could make it, I guess we can."

"All right." Detrick turned his head to Lieutenant Martell. "Martell, you take ten men and work your way up-country for about half a mile. Leave your horses on the rim with one man guarding them and take the others down into the canyon on foot. Find yourself some cover within easy rifle range of the bottom." Feeling the coolness of the predawn air, he stared eastward, looking for some sign of light. He saw none but he knew it would not be long in coming. He pulled out his watch and lit a match so he could see the hands. He said, "It's five after four now. I want you in position at four-thirty. You've got a watch, haven't you?"

"Yes, sir." Martell rode back to the troop and softly called out ten names. He rode away up the rim of the canyon and the men followed him.

Detrick was thinking about all the military strategy he had ever learned. He knew he was weakening himself dangerously. He had already left two troops behind. Now he was in the process of dividing his remaining troop into three separate forces, none of which was going to be strong enough to decisively defeat even the twenty Apaches he knew to be on the canyon floor. If those twenty had been reinforced then he might be leading the men of C Troop to certain death.

For a moment he hesitated, wanting to call Lieutenant Martell back. His own judgment told him he'd be better off taking the entire troop down this slope. But it was characteristic of him to be indecisive and now he hesitated a little bit too long. It was too late to call Martell back by the time he had decided to do so and he knew he would look foolish if he sent someone after him.

But he didn't have to divide this force. When he and Hazelthorne returned to the troop, he said, "The rest of you wait here. We'll all go down this slope."

Hazelthorne stared at him in disbelief. He couldn't see Detrick's face but he could plainly hear the self-doubt in Detrick's voice. He knew he had no business questioning the colonel's judgment. He also knew that if the lower end of the canyon was left open, the Apaches would all escape that way. Finally he asked, "Colonel, aren't you going to stop up the canyon on the lower end?"

Detrick's face reddened and he was glad it was too dark

for the men to see. He said, "I don't want to divide my force any more than I already have."

"But, Colonel . . ."

"Sergeant! That's enough!" Detrick's voice was sharp.

Hazelthorne knew there was no use arguing. Detrick was unsure of himself and, as usual, indecisive. He didn't know what he ought to do, but once he had committed himself as he had now, pride would prevent any backing down. Especially before an enlisted man.

Hazelthorne also knew that the success of Garcia's plan depended on stopping up the canyon at both ends. The force going down this slope wasn't supposed to engage the Apaches head to head. It was only supposed to drive them either up or down the canyon or both. The Apaches would figure on putting their original ambush plan into effect. They wouldn't know that a similar ambush was waiting for them.

Hazelthorne eased his horse through the men to the outer edge of the group. There were nearly forty men here, counting noncoms and the colonel.

Suddenly Hazelthorne was scared. If Detrick let the Apaches escape down the canyon, then those same Apaches would return on foot along the slopes and fire down into the cavalrymen, driving them up the canyon where they could be bottled up and slaughtered one by one.

Hazelthorne had never deliberately disobeyed an order in his life. But he was going to disobey one now. No matter what the consequences. Even if he spent the next ten years in an army prison, which he probably would, he was going to do what Garcia had told him to do.

Silently he rode along the edge of the troop, touching a man here and there, indicating they were to follow him. When he had ten men, he rode silently away into the darkness, holding a hand to his mouth to indicate he wanted complete silence, beckoning with the other hand.

Silently he prayed the colonel wouldn't see them leaving. He was grateful for the darkness, grateful that by now the moon had sunk behind the horizon in the west. Now a dozen yards separated them from the main group. Now twenty yards. He held his breath, hoping some damn fool wouldn't call out and ask where they were going so quietly.

Fifty yards now, and Hazelthorne began to breathe a little easier. When two hundred yards separated them from the main group of nearly thirty men, he touched his horse's sides with his heels and the animal broke into a trot.

Not until they were nearly a quarter mile away did one of the men speak. It was Buck Hutchcroft. He said softly, "You'll be an old man before you get out of the stockade."

Sourly Hazelthorne said, "Better alive in the stockade than dead down on that canyon floor."

They reached a place approximately half a mile from where they had left Detrick and the main body of the troop. Hazelthorne dismounted. He said, "Jenkins, you stay here with the horses. Make damn sure none of them get away."

Jenkins was silent an instant. Relief that he would not have to fight washed through his mind like a cleansing flood. But he heard himself saying, to his own horror, "Sergeant, couldn't I go down into the canyon with you?"

"Why?"

Jenkins knew there was no use beating around the bush. He hoped his voice wouldn't shake, and because he did, it came out louder than he had intended that it should. "I ain't never seen any action before, Sergeant, and I'm scared. If I stay up here, I'll spend my whole damn life being scared."

Hazelthorne was silent a moment. He would rather have left Jenkins up here because Jenkins was green and there-

fore not completely dependable. But he could remember
how he had felt himself on the eve of his first action a long
time ago. He growled, "All right. But by God, I'll tell you
something and all the rest of you too. If one of you fires a
gun before I give the word, I'm personally going to blow
that man's head off."

Nobody said anything. "Samuels, you stay here with the
horses."

The men dismounted, leaving the reins dragging so the
horses could graze but ensuring they would not stray far.
Hazelthorne led the way to the canyon rim. There was
rimrock here, and the drop was about twenty feet. For an
instant he felt panicky. What if he was unable to find the
draw Garcia had shown him in time? But he knew it was
close and he led his men east along the rim.

He found it less than fifty yards away, and led the way
down, cautioning the men not to dislodge any more rocks
than necessary. He thought they were far enough away from
the Indian camp so that the sounds would not be heard, but
he had no assurance there wasn't an Indian sentry down
there someplace.

He had used up almost fifteen minutes arguing with Detrick, gathering his men, and coming this far. That left him
less than fifteen minutes to get to the bottom of the canyon
and get his men into position.

As always, going into a scrap, the blood was pumping
hard and fast in his veins. There were slight tremors in his
hands. But unlike Jenkins, Hazelthorne knew how he was
going to react when the battle actually began.

One of the men lost his footing and slid into Hazelthorne.
He stopped the man and cautioned again, "Careful, damn
it! You want them to be waiting for us down there?"

Again, as silently as possible, the men worked their way

toward the bottom. At last Hazelthorne saw it, a twisting, narrow stream bed in which no water ran. He hunkered down and let the others catch up with him. There was the faintest tinge of gray in the sky, but he could hear nothing from up the canyon and therefore knew Detrick and the men with him had not yet started down. Hazelthorne guessed, knowing the colonel, that Detrick would wait until it was light enough to see the entire slope before he started down.

Glancing around, he spotted several rocks large enough to hide a man. He pointed, sending a man to each. Over on the other side were more rocks large enough and he directed men to each of them. Hutchcroft remained with him, and now Hutchcroft whispered, "See that pile of dead brush down there that a flood washed up some time or another? How about letting me go down there?"

Hazelthorne stared at the piled-up, tangled mass of dead cactus, brush, and tree branches. It was maybe three feet high and six or eight feet across. He said, "If they overrun it, you're dead. You know that, don't you?"

"I know. But from there I can kill twice as many as I would up here."

Hazelthorne hesitated. He knew how valuable a man could be down behind that pile of brush. The Apaches would have no way of knowing only one man was there. It was possible Hazelthorne would either stop them altogether or halt them long enough for the riflemen on the slopes to take a deadly toll. He nodded, and handed Hutchcroft his revolver and ammunition pouch. "You'll need this more than I will."

Hutchcroft took them and stuffed the gun into his belt. Carrying his carbine and the ammunition pouch for the revolver, he slid on down the slope, careful to stay on the slope until he was directly opposite the pile of brush so that he would leave no tracks in the sandy, dry bed of the stream.

The sky was now wholly gray. Hazelthorne was ready, and now that he was he had time to think about what Colonel Detrick was going to do to him when this was over with. It wasn't pleasant. He was guilty of rank insubordination. The very least that would happen to him would be the loss of his stripes. The worst would be years in an army prison.

But he didn't regret what he had done. Angrily he put the worry out of his mind and concentrated instead on the twisting canyon floor stretching away to his right. He could understand why someone had named it Soda Creek. Alkali had turned the banks of the dry stream a splotchy white.

Suddenly, sounding like firecrackers in the distance, he heard the crackle of rifle fire. His voice rolled out across the canyon, bellowing, "Stay under cover, now, so they won't see you until it's too late. And don't fire until I do! We want 'em right under us before we open up!" He settled himself more comfortably behind his rock. As an afterthought he yelled, "And take your time, like you was on the rifle range. I want every bullet to get an Indian!"

Now, he knew, there was nothing to do but wait.

# CHAPTER 19

Colonel Detrick waited until the entire sky was gray, until he could see the bottom of the canyon and the many, many sleeping forms. Garcia had been right, he thought. The Indians who had been in the village through which they had passed had joined the others and an ambush had, indeed, been planned. Today his three troops would have ridden down into this canyon and followed the Indians' trail. They'd have ridden right into the diabolically planned ambush, and if more than a handful had escaped, it would have been a miracle.

He looked around, uneasy suddenly about the smallness of his force. "Where the hell is Hazelthorne?"

Corporal Delaney was the one upon whom his glance fell. "Where is he, Corporal?" Detrick repeated.

Delaney's face turned white, but he knew there was no use trying to lie. He said, "Hazelthorne took about ten men and rode down the canyon, sir."

Detrick felt his face getting red. He had been deliberately disobeyed, and when he got his hands on Hazelthorne the man was going to be damned sorry for it. But it was time, though, and there was no use thinking about Hazelthorne's disobedience now. He raised an arm, waved it forward, and gave the command to advance. He couldn't help believing he was riding to his death and taking these men along with him.

In first dawn light, he could see the trail the Indians had made going down into the canyon. With his horse sliding on his haunches, ears laid back and eyes rolling with fright, Detrick forced him down the slope, raising a huge cloud of dust that partially hid the men following.

He discovered, to his surprise, that anger had mostly dissolved both his fear and his uncertainty. Shaver had planned to lead this entire command to their deaths, though why he carried such a hate Detrick had no idea. Garcia had gone ahead, against orders, to try and rescue Stephanie and that angered Detrick too, because in the end it would be Garcia who would look like a hero, both in Stephanie's eyes and in the eyes of the men. If any of them survived. And to cap it off, Hazelthorne had flagrantly disobeyed a direct order and had taken ten men and gone off on his own, perhaps dooming the thirty men who remained. It was enough to make any man furious, enough to make Detrick forget that he'd never had any real combat experience.

They were about a third of the way down the slope before a shout lifted on the valley floor. It was taken up immediately by half a hundred others. Sleeping Indians leaped to their feet, snatched up their weapons, and began to fire at the cavalry sliding their horses down the slope. Detrick bawled, "Hold your fire!" knowing that if his men got panicky and began shooting now they'd kill more of their own than Indians.

The Apaches must have thought the entire three troops of cavalry were coming down the slope because dust hid all but the score or so riding in the front. After firing twenty or thirty rounds, without visible effect, they broke and ran, about half up the canyon, the other half down. Detrick couldn't see the Indians' horse herd because of a bend in the canyon, but he could see the enormous cloud of dust they raised as they stampeded away.

He realized, with some amazement, that Garcia's plan had worked. But even more heady than that realization was the one that no longer did he feel either indecisive or afraid.

Garcia waited, crouched behind his rock, until he saw Detrick and his troops come off the lip of the canyon rim and start down the slope. In another instant, he thought, the Indians would awake and when they did there would be nothing but confusion on the canyon floor. Looking at the towering cloud of dust raised by the colonel and the few men immediately behind him, Garcia realized that the Indians would have no way of knowing Detrick had only thirty men. They would assume, naturally enough, that he had all three troops with him.

But even in the confusion, a blue tunic was going to stand out like a sore thumb. Swiftly he slipped out of it. His red underwear was sweat-stained and faded, and he decided it would be better than the dead-white skin of his torso.

An Indian shouted—the one who had been standing by the fire. Another awoke, and another, and suddenly the whole valley floor was alive with moving Indians, who hurriedly snatched up guns and began to fire haphazardly at the soldiers sliding down the slope.

Garcia himself was up and running along the slope at a diagonal, toward the spot of white he had noticed earlier. The Indians, their attention rooted on the troopers, apparently didn't notice him. He reached the canyon floor just as the Apaches gave up trying to shoot at the troops and began scattering to right and left, up the canyon and down.

The spot of white he had seen in the darkness was indeed

the two women. They were both sitting up now, staring with utter surprise at what was taking place.

They saw Garcia at the same instant Garcia saw three Indians who had left the others and were running straight toward the two women. He roared, "Get up and run!"

Upon their doing so depended their slim chance of survival, because the Apaches were closer to them than Garcia was. He saw one of the Indians, older than the other two, turn his head and give an order. Instantly one of the younger Indians veered toward him.

Garcia knew he had no time to struggle with the Indian. And he knew he didn't dare risk missing the man with his first shot.

He therefore slid to an instant stop, dropped to one knee, and, holding his service revolver in both hands, took careful aim.

Seeing the muzzle of the gun staring so implacably at him, the Indian tried, too late, to drop to the ground. Garcia fired.

The bullet took the Apache not in the chest, where it had been aimed, but in the throat instead. He pitched forward and lay on his face, full length, twitching as his life blood flowed away onto the dusty, thirsty ground.

Garcia didn't want to make sure the man was dead; knowing he had been hit was enough. He was up immediately, running once more toward the two women, who were fleeing now, and the two Indians closing so rapidly upon them.

Stephanie, hardly recognizable to Garcia, ran easily and without panic, for all that she was not as swift as the man pursuing her. The other woman seemed completely hysterical. She kept looking over her shoulder, paying little attention to the terrain.

Her foot caught on a rock lying half buried in the sand and she sprawled headlong. Garcia knew he'd never reach her before the Apache did. He knew he might stop once more, steady his gun, and try to bring the Apache down. His thoughts and the decision he made were like lightning and even as he made that decision he knew there would be many times in his later life when he would look back and regret what he had done or failed to do.

But the Apache was sixty or seventy yards away. He was in a direct line between Garcia and the prostrate woman, now screaming hysterically as she saw the savage approaching her, rifle poised to smash her skull.

Garcia did not stop. He raced after the Apache pursuing Stephanie, running as he had never run in his life before. The Indian was gaining on Stephanie rapidly because she was impeded by her skirts even though she was holding them up as much as possible.

Garcia heard the fallen ranch woman scream, but he didn't look around. He'd been forced to make an awful choice and, even if he'd known neither woman, his choice had been the only one possible. He'd elected to try saving the woman he had the best chance to save.

The Apache was now less than a dozen yards behind Stephanie Detrick and Garcia bawled, "Stephanie! Turn one way or the other! You're in my line of fire!"

His shout and her recognition of his voice nearly made her stop. Then, easily and with only that one slight break in stride, she veered sharply right toward the canyon wall.

Once more Garcia, only a dozen yards behind the Indian, dropped to one knee. He raised his revolver with both hands, sighted carefully, and pulled the trigger.

The bullet took the Apache in the shoulder and its weight and impact spun the man around. Momentarily the Indian forgot Stephanie, giving her time to race onward and begin to climb the slope.

Garcia was up instantly, running toward the wounded Indian. The man had a rifle and now he swung it awkwardly, forced to control it mostly with his uninjured arm and hand.

No time now to drop to one knee and shoot again. There was not even time to raise his revolver and fire on the run. Garcia saw the rifle muzzle come into line and he did what the other Indian he'd shot only a few seconds before had done. He dived forward, falling. The rifle roared, emitting a huge cloud of black powder smoke, the grains of which stung Garcia's face and nearly blinded him. But he felt no bullet impact and he knew that somehow, miraculously, he had been missed.

He also knew he was appallingly vulnerable stretched out this way at the wounded Indian's feet. He rolled, even as the Apache swung his empty gun. The butt struck the ground where Garcia's head had been an instant before. The wooden stock smashed, but the Indian still had the barrel to use as a club and he lunged toward Garcia, raising it for another blow.

Garcia raised his revolver and thumbed the hammer back, hoping the muzzle hadn't become plugged with sand when he fell. He fired, and immediately afterward tried to roll and scramble away from that murderous iron club in the Apache's hands.

The rifle struck the ground, once more missing Garcia by inches. The Indian fell across Garcia, and he fought like a tiger to free himself. But he was fighting an inert mass. The Indian was dead.

No time to pause, no time even to catch his breath. The valley was swarming with Indians. Detrick's force had by now reached the canyon floor.

Garcia leaped to his feet and sprinted in the direction Stephanie had gone. He saw the Apache who had killed the other woman running toward him, trying to cut him off.

Garcia couldn't remember how many times he had fired his revolver and there wasn't time for reloading now. Dropping to one knee for a third time, he steadied the sights on the approaching Apache and when the man was less than a dozen feet away fired.

The man pitched forward. Garcia got up and ran again. He knew there was a good chance that the Apaches would notice that Detrick had only thirty men. He knew that when they did they'd stand and fight instead of fleeing into the ambushes set at both ends of the canyon just beyond their camp. If they did that, the troopers, outnumbered six to one, were bound to be wiped out.

But he still had Stephanie to worry about. He was damned if he was going to leave her now and let her be killed. He ran after her and reached her as she crouched down behind a spindly clump of brush.

There was sheer terror in her eyes. In her trembling body and mouth were the beginnings of hysteria. Garcia knew he couldn't rely on her to remain here behind this brush. He knew if she showed herself she'd become a target for every Apache who happened to see her.

Once more his decision was quickly made. His fist made a short, savage arc. It connected with Stephanie's jaw and she slumped and lay sprawled on the slope as if she was dead.

Returning toward the milling battle, Garcia hoped he hadn't broken her jaw. He also hoped she would someday forgive him for what he had done. But he was certain of one thing. Only if Stephanie Detrick appeared to be dead would the Apaches leave her alone.

The men of C Troop now were bunched, still mounted,

most with empty guns they were trying to reload, awkwardly because of their horses' terrified plunging. Detrick sat his horse, firing with his revolver, paying no apparent attention to the men.

At a dead run, Garcia roared, "Dismount and fight on foot! Take cover behind those dead horses! Damn it, make every bullet count!"

What had started out as a complete surprise and promised to be a slaughter of the Indians, had now turned around the other way. The Apaches were no longer fleeing. Realizing how few soldiers had come riding down the canyon slope, they had stopped running and turned to fight.

Hearing Garcia's voice, the troopers dismounted hastily. There were five or six horses lying dead and they dived behind the carcasses for cover. Detrick glanced toward Garcia, then looked at the men, who had followed Garcia's orders, ignoring his. He bawled, "Get back on those horses! Charge!"

Not a man obeyed. Detrick sat there uncertainly for a moment, the only clear target for a hundred or more Indians.

In the next moment he was literally riddled where he sat. His horse, shot through the neck, folded forward and collapsed onto his side. Neither horse nor man moved again.

Behind the downed horses, the remaining men of C Troop were now calmly reloading and firing. A few Indians fell. But there were not enough troopers to fight two hundred well-armed Indians. It was only a matter of time before they would be overrun.

# CHAPTER 20

Lying behind a dead horse with a trooper on either side of him, Garcia reloaded his revolver, then steadied it on the horse's still-warm side and began firing at the Indians. The Indians' charge, which had begun when they killed Detrick, faltered before the deadly, if scattered fire coming from the concealed troopers. They fell back, looking for cover, finding precious little of it on the flat canyon floor.

Garcia's gun was hot as he reloaded it again. At least, he thought, they had gained a momentary respite. The trouble was, the Indians would regroup and charge again. They would realize how few of the soldiers remained. They would realize that the soldiers did not have repeating carbines. They would draw a volley and then, while the troopers tried hastily to reload, would charge. This position would be over-run. Every man would be killed.

Frantically, Garcia's mind searched for a way out of the seemingly hopeless predicament. He could find none. Out-numbered more than six to one, there was simply no hope they could turn things around. The only hope that existed, and it was a slim one, was that they could somehow hold out until the other two troops arrived. But that was probably two or three hours away. There was practically no chance that they could hold out that long.

Desperately Garcia roared, "Don't all fire at once. Every

other man is to hold his fire until the men next to him have reloaded their guns."

Almost immediately the gunfire slackened. Garcia glanced toward the place he had left Stephanie. He could see her still lying on the slope. No Indians were near to her. The ranch woman's body lay on the canyon floor, awkwardly sprawled and dead. Garcia felt a stab of guilt over the unfortunate woman's death but he knew he could have done no more than he had done. He could not have saved both women no matter how desperately he had tried. And if he had tried to save them both, he would probably have ended up saving neither one.

The Apaches were massing now, being exhorted by one of their number who was older than the rest. They were getting ready for a charge. Garcia knew his men might get fifteen or twenty of them, but that kind of loss wouldn't even slow them down.

He shouted, "They're going to charge! Every other man is to hold his fire until I give the word!"

Nobody answered him and he didn't know how well they would obey when they saw a solid wall of savage, half-naked Apaches charging them. He didn't suppose it really mattered very much anyway. They were going to be overrun. They all were going to be killed. Swiftly he reloaded his revolver, promising himself he would get six of the charging Indians before they got him.

The Indian leader raised both arms. He roared something in Apache that Garcia did not understand. Carrying their rifles at the ready, the Apaches suddenly swarmed toward the barricaded handful of troopers.

Garcia roared once more, "Hold your fire until I give the word!" He wanted the toll of the first volley to be devastating, an Apache for every bullet fired if possible. Now the

Apaches were only fifty yards away, crouched low and running hard.

Garcia opened his mouth to give the word to fire. But he never issued the command. Suddenly, behind him, more sweetly than any sound he had ever heard in his life before, came the clear, strong bugle notes of the "Charge."

He turned his head and glanced up toward the canyon rim. What he saw turned his despair of a moment before into a surge of hope. Plunging down the canyon slope came the horses and men of troops B and K, and behind the leaders rose an enormous cloud of dust. They weren't due yet but there they were. Thank God Schofield and Healy had used a little initiative.

He glanced back at the charging Indians. Their charge had slowed. Some of them had stopped. All were looking up toward that mass of descending cavalrymen. Now was the time. Garcia roared, "Fire!"

Raggedly the volley rang out. Eight or ten Apaches dropped. The entire line had stopped now and Garcia knew another volley would turn them back. He roared, "Odd men! Fire!"

The second volley roared out, and another half dozen Indians dropped. And suddenly the Apaches broke. Turning, they ran, scattering as they did.

Now they did what they were supposed to have done earlier. In complete panic, they broke, running hard, for what they believed was the safety of the upper and lower canyon, probably meaning to implement their original ambush plan by climbing the canyon walls and concealing themselves behind rocks from which they could fire down into the pursuing troopers' ranks.

Garcia's men reloaded swiftly and threw another volley at the retreating Indians. And then the mounted troops reached the canyon floor and split, B Troop pursuing the Indians that had run up the canyon, K Troop pursuing those who had headed down.

Garcia got to his feet. He was dusty and bloody from his two wounds, but he felt better than he had in a long time. Victory had been plucked from disaster. Stephanie was alive and the losses to the men had been very small. Given time to rest, both horses and men would be able to make it safely back to the fort.

He walked to Colonel Detrick, knelt, and satisfied himself that Detrick was dead. For a while when Detrick had been leading his men down the slope, Garcia had thought his assessment of Detrick had been wrong. But faced with disaster on the canyon floor, Detrick had panicked, stopped thinking, and paid for his panic with his life.

By now, both Indians and pursuing troopers had disappeared. As the Indians apparently came abreast of the ambushes laid earlier, Garcia heard the faint crackle of rifle fire.

He turned. "Corporal Delaney, take some men and look to the wounded."

"Yes, sir."

Garcia walked toward Stephanie, still lying motionless behind the stunted clump of brush low on the slope of the canyon wall. As he reached her, she stirred and moaned.

He knelt and stared down at her. Her face was blistered and covered with scabs where blisters had broken and begun to heal. Her hair was stringy, bleached and made brittle by the sun. She seemed thin and helpless lying there.

Her eyes opened and she looked up at him, and suddenly Garcia could see and remember her as she had been before the war. He said, "It's all right. It's over and you're safe. I'm sorry I had to hit you, but I had to make the Indians think that you were dead."

Her eyes stared at him unblinkingly. "My husband. Is he . . . ?"

"He's dead."

Her steady glance was disconcerting. But there was something there, something he could not exactly define but which he understood. It would be a long way back for them. But they would make it. And they would be together in the end.